Parlous Angels

Parlous Angels

stories

Ed Southern

9/27/09

Press 53
Winston-Salem, NC

Press 53
PO Box 30314
Winston-Salem, NC 27130

First Edition

This book is a complete work of fiction. All names, characters, places and incidents are products of the author's imagination. Any resemblances to actual events, places or persons, living or dead, are coincidental.

Cover design by Kevin Watson

Cover photo, "Workmen Put a New Roof on Single Sisters' House," Courtesy of Old Salem Museums & Gardens.

"The Survivors" first appeared in *Main Street Rag*, Summer 2006.

Printed on acid-free paper

ISBN: 978-0-9824416-4-0

for Corbyn and Molly

Contents

Primogeniture 1

The Parlous Angel 9

Why John Gardiner Learned to Gamble 15

The Donnoha Beast 29

Squirrel Hunting 41

Symbolon 47

The Battler 55

The Wrecks of the Reconstruction 63

War Orphan 71

The Survivors 83

Intercession 89

Baptists on the Edge 93

At a Gypsy Camping Place 101

Study Bible 115

The Postpunk Chronicles 123

At the End of Ocean Boulevard 139

The Death of John Gardiner 149

The Playground of the Fearless 159

Primogeniture

The Danney Tree Company's driveway was sort of hidden, flanked by honeysuckle and kudzu, cutting back at a more-than-right angle from Craighead Road. Will Adams found it, though. He found it and followed it through a sunburned yard as it curved twice and ended on the far side of the Danney Tree garage. Behind the garage was an open-ended shed with vast bay doors and a vaulting roof. The truly heavy machinery got parked there at the end of each day. Will parked his truck near the end of the shed.

Will always jumped out of the truck quickly, in a burst, in part because he was eager to work hard, but mostly because he was thin and nervous and light. When he went to a new stop, like the Danney Tree Company, he'd leap from the cab and then have to stop awkwardly. He'd have to try to figure out where he was supposed to be, which door he was supposed to use, whether he was supposed to go inside at all. When he stopped and stood this time he saw a pile of massive parts lying halfway down the side of the shed. He saw a cherry picker with a big boom crane in the bay closest to the garage, sitting above a pool of some fluid. A man came from behind the cherry-picker and stared at Will.

The man could do a fair job passing for a tree, Will thought. He could, in fact, have been the personification of Danney Tree, made flesh, pleased to meet you. At least six-foot-five, with a bulk to match, he stood stock-still and stared at Will from behind a ball of bushy hair and bushy beard. Will couldn't see the man's eyes.

"You got a pick-up for Brake Service?" Will called across the shed.

The man didn't answer, but at least, after a moment, he moved. He lowered his head and walked a few slow steps toward the near side of the shed. He stopped suddenly and raised a huge, filthy hand and the filthy grease rag it held. From out of his beard he alliterated, "That's them there."

Will was afraid of that.

This was the second summer that driving the parts truck had been Will's second choice of a job. Last summer he and some friends were going to go to Alaska and work on a fishing boat. His father, reminding Will that he'd spent his last ocean voyage throwing his guts up, instead offered him $7 an hour to run the parts truck while the regular driver recuperated. The regular driver had gotten himself t-boned on Tryon Street. This summer Will had applied for a grant to write a novel in verse about baseball, in 18 chapters, with each chapter representing a half-inning. When his application was rejected his father offered him $8 an hour to help out in the warehouse. Then the new parts driver quit and Will got back behind the wheel. He liked that better than the warehouse, anyway. In there the scenery never changed and he never saw the sun, and the dusty, oily air in the warehouse made his acne flare up.

After Danney Tree pointed, Will climbed into the truck and drove a little ways back down the driveway. He braked, put the truck in reverse, and backed it slowly closer to the pile of massive parts he'd already seen. When the sales counter had beeped him they'd said go to Danney Tree Company and pick up two rotors, two brake drums, and a few brake shoes. They had not said pick up two rotors and two brake drums off of some kind of tree-devouring monstrosity that's probably big enough to keep God awake at night. A single brake drum from a standard 18-wheeler was about 80 pounds of solid steel, shaped like a bowl with a 10-inch hole at the bottom. A rotor off the same 18-wheeler was about the same size as the drum, a little bit heavier, and vaguely shaped like a five-pointed star. They were heavy-duty parts, but Will could handle them. Each of the bad boys he stared at now probably weighed more than he did. True, he didn't weigh very much, but the point was still valid—these sons-a-bitches were big.

Will opened the double doors at the back of the truck. The truck bed stood somewhere between his knees and his crotch. Will scratched a spot beside his left eye and wondered how he would know for sure if he got a hernia. He pulled his leather gloves from his hip pocket and slid them on. He squatted next to one of the drums.

With one hand on the outer edge and one hand in the center hole, Will picked the drum up, grunted, pivoted, grunted again as he did, leaned back for elevation since he could not lift his arms, and set the drum on the edge of the truck bed. He climbed into the truck, to the other side of the drum, and dragged it up to the cage that separated the bed from the cab. Bent double, he climbed out, straightened his back, and squatted beside the next drum. The second one seemed to go a little easier than the first, knowledge being power and all. He climbed out of the truck and caught his breath.

He stared sadly at the rotors. Whatever vehicle these were for, it wasn't just bigger than a semi, but also had a different wheel structure. These rotors were half-again as large as the brake drums, and so would have to weigh twice as much. Will breathed deeply, and admitted to himself that he didn't think he could lift one of these. He looked around the shed. He could not see Danney Tree. He adjusted his balls. He'd lived a good life. He'd managed to avoid, one way or another, anything really difficult. He'd had responsible parents, teachers who recognized and encouraged ability, comfortable homes, plentiful food. He'd fought his share of playground fights, but his life for the most part had been peaceful. He hated it. Twenty years spent knocking on wood, waiting for the boot to drop. In place of great trials, he was left to this small test: obvious, kind of pathetic, and still a job that had to be done. He took a deep breath.

He shoved his skinny fingers beneath one edge, digging into the dirt to get good and under the metal. When he had a kind of grip, something like leverage, he pulled up on that side of the rotor. The long tendons from his wrists to his elbows popped out taut beneath his skin; his biceps turned small and round. He was pretty sure he was making a strange face.

One afternoon as they drove home Will's father had told the story of how Will's grandfather came to play football.

"Here he was, new in school, new in Winston-Salem, which back then was the big city for all those mountain boys. So now he had every boy on the football team and every coach at Hanes High School clucking like a chicken every time he walked by, just because his mother had made him quit the team."

Will remembered every story anyone had ever told him about his grandfather.

"So he started going to practice again and he and Granddaddy just didn't tell Grandma," Jim Adams continued. "I don't know. Guess she thought he might get hurt and not be able to work or something."

Will pulled and heaved until the rotor stood on its side. He spun it in place until he had it aimed at the back of the truck. He pushed it from the top, rolling it forward, but the star-like points and the rotor's top-heavy build denied it equilibrium. Will had to work hard, holding tight to the sides and straining, to keep the rotor from falling over. When he reached the truck he spun the rotor again until he could lean it back against the bumper. He caught his breath and stretched his arms.

Will seemed to recall being ten and wanting to quit baseball when his father first told him how his grandfather started working when he was eight. The summer he was eight, Will's grandfather walked three miles with his father to a construction site, where he spent all day every day toting a wheelbarrow full of bricks or blocks or mortar.

He was never a big man, but when his hands grabbed hold of something that something was held. He was offered scholarships to play college ball, but he turned them down to go to work laying brick. He joined the Army after the war started, married his high school sweetheart, saw his first son safely born, shipped out two weeks later, landed at Normandy, won the Bronze Star, came home and laid brick until he died, that simple.

Will squatted behind the truck, behind the rotor, and put his hands as solidly as he could on two of the points. He began to lift. He could feel the strain of ligaments from his fingers to his neck, and could feel the narrow cords of muscle bulge. The rotor rose off the ground, enough that Will could put his knee beneath it for support. He rested for a second. Then he lowered his body, his center of gravity, and pushed on the rotor from below. The metal scraped against the chrome of the bumper and the steel of the truck, before it reached the tipping point and crashed into the bed. The rear of the truck shuddered and lurched. A lug nut on the rotor's lower end caught Will in the thigh as it rose; he could feel blood begin to trickle beneath his work pants. He turned to face the second rotor.

One afternoon before they left the shop Will's father said something that Will couldn't understand. While Will sat on the sales counter, while they waited for the sales report to print, his father talked to the office manager about the deaths of loved ones. Throughout the shop, parents were old and sick, and funerals were coming quickly that summer.

Will Adams's grandfather had never been old or sick. His heart stopped one Sunday morning on the steps in front of his church. He had helped build that church, not with his money but with his hands, brick by brick. He was not yet fifty and his oldest son was engaged to be married.

Will's father, still not aware of how Will paid attention, told the office manager, "The day my father died, I lost control of my world."

Will had long thought of that day as the day his father took control, shouldering the world and his family. Every now and then he'd anticipate facing such a day himself, and then he'd knock on wood. He thought of the day his grandfather died as the day his father stopped being the boy Jamie Adams, once and for all, and became the man even his own mother now called Jim. Will himself was only Will to himself and to his classmates and teachers at college; Will's parents and anyone who knew Will's parents still called him Billy. Will Adams was still his grandfather's name, not really his. His name was a gift to honor his grandfather, a gift he had not yet deserved.

By now Will felt drained, by his full day's work and by the drums and the first rotor. He looked at his watch, which read four o'clock. He was breathing hard and staring glumly at the last rotor. Through the corner of his eye he saw Danney Tree's hairy head watching him over the hood of the cherry-picker. Will hunkered down.

One evening when Will was eight he brought home a release form for Pop Warner football. His father had coached Pop Warner teams for years, had coached a team that won the national championship. Will knew he was small, slow and clumsy, but he had never considered that he wouldn't play when he was old enough. The minimum weight was 70 pounds and Will only weighed 55. The weight requirement would be waived, however, if Will's father signed the release.

"I'm not going to tell you you can't play," his father said, sitting in his chair in the den after dinner. "But I want you to know what you're getting yourself into." He told Will about the practices he ran, and he didn't leave out one hit, one sprint, one drill. He told him about boys, big boys, good athletes, throwing up after or even in the middle of practice. He told him about boys, big boys, good athletes, breaking their arms and ribs and collarbones, just in practice, much less in a game. He described all the damage one boy could do to another. "And since you're not that fast, they'd have you playing down on the line with the really big kids." As he spoke Will began to have doubts. As his father finished Will decided he'd better wait. His father nodded. "I think that'd be the best thing. Maybe you'll hit a growth spurt before next season."

As the rotor rose from the ground Will felt his biceps like to rip from the bone. Now the weight was no longer taxing or tiring or burdening him; now the weight was breaking him. He held his breath as he struggled the rotor away from the earth. He had the rotor on the lip of the truck bed, with just a little farther to push. He felt the strength leave his arms and legs. He was afraid he could no longer even hold the rotor in place, and that all of that steel would crash on his frail and weakened limbs.

He was stuck beneath the rotor, breathing hard, unable to move, when he felt the warm, comforting surge run through him. He felt the reassurance, the familiarity of his uncontrollable, overwhelming, irresponsible anger. Why the fuck didn't they tell me about this, he thought, and why the fuck isn't that big hairy fuck over there helping? He felt his anger fill him, that fluttering rage that twisted his face, that he hoped would someday change him into a berserker, Achilles, a war-raged Cuchullainn, the Incredible Hulk, anything other than the nothing he was now. He cussed himself and the rotor, spitting out the words in not much more than a whisper, "Fuck me, come on. Goddamn it. Come on." He felt the anger contort him, the anger he saw on his father's face all the many times Will had made him ashamed. The anger launched him into the rotor, which rose and tipped and fell, coming to rest in the bed of the truck.

Gasping for air, his arms warm and weightless, Will went to get the brake shoes scattered around the site of the pile. He tossed them onto and around the drums and rotors. Danney Tree was still watching him.

He spoke again. "You're kinda small to be doing this job, ain't you?"

Will dwelt on his anger for a moment, looked at Danney Tree, and decided he'd best take that for a compliment. "I seem to do all right," he said. He took off the leather gloves and started up the parts truck.

Back at the loading dock Will got some help unloading the parts from Danney Tree Company onto the cart. Duane asked him, "You get that big ol' boy out there to help you load these?" and Will got to answer, "No."

"Dang, Billy," Duane said. He rolled the cart down to the shop, and when Duane passed Mark and Keith and Hobart, Will could see him talking, pointing at the rotors, pointing at Will. Will checked the board to see where he'd go next.

As they drove home that afternoon, Jim Adams said, "Well, only one more week of this and you're done."

"You sure you don't need me to work next week?"

"Nah. Kyle's coming back next week."

"I could help out in the warehouse."

"Nah. You take some time off before school."

They had to wait to turn onto Highway 51. A truck was coming out of the feed store. They had driven around Charlotte to avoid the traffic. They hadn't talked much on the way. After he made the turn, though, Jim Adams told Will a story about his father, a story Will had never heard before: when he was a teenager, having no money to buy a car, he built himself one out of parts from the junkyard. That story led to another. Down the highway, through the middle of the bedroom towns, Jim told his son things he'd never told before, as if sharing his most precious estate. The stories continued until they re-entered Charlotte.

"You're going to be busy this week," Will's father said.

"I know."

"Before you leave, I want you to get done everything that needs doing."

"I will."

The Parlous Angel

Thirty years ago, no lone deputy, armed or not, would have set one foot in Mother McCaskill's house. Michael Hawkins, bulging holster on his hip and warm rifle in his hands, didn't know that, but he did swallow hard as he passed through her door. He remembered the stories his mother had told him about Mother McCaskill. Thirty years ago the stories meant more, and more stories were told.

When Mother McCaskill came to town, whole gardens died. Mother McCaskill walked past and the dogs on the street took to howling. Mother McCaskill set her evil eye upon you, and the next day you might wake up lame, if you woke up at all.

Thirty-three years ago Mother McCaskill walked down out of the Blue Ridge, alongside a Mister McCaskill who already looked wrung out. Behind her trailed thirteen children, some of whom were her own. The others were children of her older children, the ones who had bred and then died, or run off to the west or to the sea, or swore they'd never come down from their mountain, but told Mother she could take the little ones so they'd neither freeze nor starve. Nobody knew how many children Mother herself had given birth to. The McCaskills were some of the last to come out of the deep hills, back when the mills first opened.

Her man died bent and gray before his first year at the mill was up. Mother McCaskill grew tomatoes and cucumbers and unfamiliar herbs in the garden in the yard behind her house. She ate the produce or sold it at a stand out by the highway, where nobody knew her, and what she made from the herbs she sold round back of her house. She sent her 13 children off to school or to the mill, and sometimes they went. Most days they ran screaming through the muddy streets, throwing rocks at whatever they thought might suffer or break, stealing what they thought they could use or enjoy, and laughing at the law and the shotguns pointed by red-faced, hollering mill hands. At home at night they howled as bad as the nearly wild dogs that Mother McCaskill had took to keeping in the yard. "To guard," she explained with a spit, never explaining what they guarded.

By the night that Michael Hawkins walked armed through her door, Mother McCaskill's 13 children had grown and gone. They'd scattered themselves throughout the mill towns up and down the Catawba valley, or found work in the factories of Winston and the foothill towns north of the Yadkin. Mother McCaskill had lived alone for years, a cat her only companion in the house constantly circled by the pack of swarming dogs. Nobody bought what she made from her herbs anymore, either because they no longer trusted them or because they didn't know what her potions were supposed to do. Nobody talked about her much anymore. Nobody had been to see her in years before Michael Hawkins walked in.

Before he approached her door, when he was standing at the far end of her street, ready to shoot, he saw her screen door swing wide, and he saw a shadowy form cross her porch and run inside her house. Hawkins started to run, but he stopped after just a few strides. He made himself walk slowly, looking from side to side, peering as far as he could see down the dark alleys between the row houses. He readied himself to shoot down an alleyway if he saw the slightest movement.

Just a few minutes before that, Hawkins had drawn aim on the Yankee Agitator at the front of the mob, and he had missed. He had watched as the crowd collapsed into a panic, falling into its center, boxed in by the wide, blank brick of the mill they had marched to and by the men now coming at them from the other three sides. Hawkins had aimed again while the Yankee Agitator, his belt wrapped around his fist with the buckle hanging loose, swung that brass buckle at the mill workers he had been organizing and ran through the path he cleared.

When the deputized men with their ax handles had charged into the mob, and then when Hawkins and the other deputies had opened fire from the shadows, all cares but survival had fallen aside. Fair wages, and safety on the floor, and shorter hours, and fairer prices at the company store didn't matter anymore, not like the room to run did, not like shelter did. Bodies in the crowd fell, and they may have been shot and dead before they hit the ground, or they might have been clubbed or pushed and then killed, shattered by the crashing weight of all those feet. Some of the stronger men grabbed hold of a woman or a child and tried to shield them from the rush, and they made themselves good targets and were shot or hit over the head with a hickory ax handle. Some of the stronger men ran past or over anything that could not protect them.

Clear of the crowd, the Yankee Agitator had run as hard as he could down the street he'd just led the marchers up. Hawkins by then had fired twice more and missed both times, and had told the laughing deputies and the deputized men, "I said I got him," and had left the dark cover and run down the mill hill after the Yankee Agitator. He had chased the Yankee's shadow across the narrow avenues and narrower yards, over the chicken-wire fences and past the darkened shacks where families huddled as far from windows as they could. He had chased the Yankee to the edge of the company town, where he'd seen the Yankee in the distance running into Mother McCaskill's, and he was chasing still when he walked, without knocking, through her door.

"You hiding that Red, Mother McCaskill?" Hawkins called out. "This here's the law. You hiding him, you need to turn him over now 'fore anybody gets hurt."

Hawkins inhaled, and the house smelled like dust, but like something else, too. The dusty smell in here wasn't the same as the flaxen air that soaked the mill hill, and something else was added. Hawkins didn't know the smell by name. He'd smelled it as a boy when he'd go to see his daddy's relations out in the country. The odor was bitter and rich. He had never thought to ask what it was.

The floorboards creaked and his shadow moved along the wall. "You got that Red here, you turn him on over to the Law, now." A faint light came from the back of the house, and Hawkins moved toward it. "You do know what a Red is, don't you, Miz McCaskill?" The glow was coming from the kitchen. "A Red's a Communist, and a atheist, and a nigger-lover. They want to shut the mill down. They want to upset the natural order of things."

Hawkins passed through the empty door frame and into the kitchen. A single flame flickered on top of a homemade candle, and behind it, from just inside its light, Mother McCaskill watched him closely and without expression. "Do they now," she said.

Her hair was solid white, but still thick, and it hung wild over her shoulders. She chewed on the stem of a corncob pipe. The look in her clear green eyes was as even and mean as that of any powerful man Hawkins had ever seen.

Hawkins adjusted his gun and spoke. "Yes, they do. Now I saw that Union man come in here. You best tell me where you got him."

"I ain't got him nowheres."

"I'll bust this place up if you make me, widow woman or not."

"I'll put her back together again when you're done."

"Do you know what a Red is?"

"A Communist, and atheist, and a nigger-lover, is what I hear."

"And you know what them words mean?"

"Do you?"

"I know what the hell the word Yankee means. That's what they are, them union men, they's Yankees sent down here to invade and conquer our God-fearing white land. Just like they put down the Cause, now they want to put down the mills."

"The cause?"

"The war, old woman, the war. The War Between the States."

"Oh. That. Which side did your people fight for?"

"That is one hell of a question to ask to a Southern man holding a gun."

Mother McCaskill shrugged. "Lots of good men fought on both sides. I remember. I was just a girl, but I remember. Do you?"

Hawkins felt a shiver start to run from the base of his spine, but he shook himself and made it go away. He told himself to forget all the stories he'd heard, the woman's age, the inviolate dark creeping in on him. He worked the lever action on his rifle, slowly, listening to the spent cartridge fall and ring on the floor, listening to the fresh round slide into the chamber. Holding the rifle low, at his waist, he turned the barrel until it pointed at Mother McCaskill.

"I always heard tell you was a witch. I didn't know you was a nasty Yankee-loving, nigger-loving traitor, too. Now you tell me where you're hiding that Red, and you tell me quick, and maybe I won't shoot you, and maybe I won't tear this house to the ground, and maybe we won't whip you out of town. Maybe we'll let you live out the few years you got left. Maybe."

Mother McCaskill took the pipe from her mouth and spat on the floor. She narrowed her clear green eyes that had never left Hawkins's face. "You know, that Red never knocked on my door, neither," she said without anger. Mother McCaskill stuck the pipe back in her mouth, and chewed it over to the side. "He went out that back door."

Hawkins could hear it now—the furious howls of her dogs when he walked in were quiet now, only mumbles and yelps. Goddamn it. "If he got away, I'm a-coming back here."

"I don't think he got away," Mother McCaskill said. She finally took her eyes off Hawkins. She stared into the candle flame. Hawkins took a deep breath as he stepped around the table. He lunged at the screen door, his rifle at his shoulder, and he fell through the door and down three feet onto the ground, which was wet and strangely sticky. The back steps his foot had reached for, the back steps at the back of every mill house he'd ever entered, weren't there. The dogs were there, and were on top of Hawkins before he could stand, and Mother McCaskill hadn't had to train them to go for the throat, because that just came natural to them.

Why John Gardiner Learned to Gamble

John Gardiner didn't believe it the first time. He raised his head from his desk and blinked at the classroom.

He believed the second time, and with his ear stinging where it had been thumped, he turned his head and looked at the boy behind him.

He knew who the boy was; everyone in Rock Springs High School did, even a freshman on his first day. The boy'd been kept back so many times that no one was sure how old he really was. The boy, his hands out and open on his desk, was grinning at John, and waiting.

John wasn't grinning. He wasn't frowning or snarling, either, as he turned and propped himself on his chair and punched the boy once in the nose.

The boy's head snapped back and his blood sprung in arcs to the desk.

A few dozen chair legs scraped across the floor as every student in the class turned around to see the fight, but the older boy kept his head down on the desk and only made small sounds.

John Gardiner, still not smiling or frowning or snarling, waited a moment, watching him, then sat back down.

The teacher, a young fellow named Mr. Crenshaw, stared at the back of the classroom in confusion. Then he recognized, and recognized his own confusion, and became angry. He set down his lecture notes and walked as loudly as he could to John's desk.

"What is this?" he yelled. He was confused again by the complete lack of answers he got. That Abernathy boy everyone had warned him about just bled from the nose and whimpered, and this other boy just sat calmly in his desk. "Well?" Crenshaw yelled. Finally the other boy looked up at him, not fast and not slow, and said, not protesting or pleading, "He shouldn't-a thumped me."

Crenshaw blinked twice at the boy. "You can't punch someone in the middle of class," came the shout that sounded like a question. John looked at the Abernathy boy and shrugged.

The rest of the class was stifling laughs. Crenshaw could hear them. He looked at the wall clock; in one minute the bell would ring. He looked at the Abernathy boy. "You," he said, "go to the bathroom. Wash that blood off. And quit whimpering." To the class he yelled, "Y'all can go on. Don't forget your homework." He put his hand on John's shoulder but did not grab. "You—come with me." He and John let the Abernathy boy out the door first, clutching his nose with both bloody hands.

The principal knew the Abernathy boy, of course, and he knew John Gardiner's family, so he told John that he hoped the next four years would not see any more of this kind of thing, and to wait next time until after school and then he could punch that boy as much as he liked. "Oh," the principal said as John was rising to leave, "you didn't hit him with your pitching hand, did you?"

"Yes, sir," John said, a little ashamed.

"You ought to know better than that, Johnny. Mr. Crenshaw, give John here a ride home; he's missed his bus by now. Give your folks my regards, Johnny."

John tried hard not to look impressed when he saw the teacher's car. The man drove one of the new B-model Fords with the V-8 engine designed by Henry Ford himself, a car John and his older brothers had read and heard and talked about but never seen. His teacher turned the engine over and John could hear the difference of the V-shape, the rumble heavier and steadier than the sound that inline cylinders made. The teacher looked at him and smiled.

"You ever seen one of these cars?"

John shrugged as he climbed into the seat. "I've read about 'em."

"Well, now you get to ride in one. Listen to that engine." He played with the throttle and the volume of the rumble. "I bought it down in Charlotte when they first rolled off the line."

You didn't buy a thing, John thought. So your daddy's rich.

"Where do you live?" Crenshaw asked.

"Out near Pumpkin Center."

"Which road?"

John thought for a moment. Nobody had ever called their road by a name, it was just their road.

"Just drive out 16. I'll show you."

Mr. Crenshaw's car sprinted out of the school parking lot and onto State Highway 16, raising gray gravel dust behind and beside.

"You a ballplayer, huh?"

"Yessir."

"What position you play?"

"Wherever they need me."

"Oh. A lot of farm boys make good ballplayers."

"My daddy's not a farmer. He owns a sawmill."

"He does what? Y'all own a sawmill?"

"Yessir."

"I didn't know there was a sawmill out in Pumpkin Center."

"Well, we got us one."

"Oh. Huh. How 'bout that."

They drove through the village, past the road that went off to the Methodist campgrounds and the river. John watched all the men who hadn't had enough cash last spring to buy seed, who didn't have enough crops to be tending now a month before harvest time, who were waiting for any kind of paying job to need to be done, that gathered around and in front of the village stores. John watched back without flinching as they watched the B-model Ford speed by.

Crenshaw looked at the men, then quickly back at the road. "I hate to admit it," he said, "but you sure helped me out today. All the other teachers warned me about that Abernathy boy. And I wasn't quite sure how I was going to handle him, truth be told. But I think you took care of him today."

The teacher laughed.

"That's not the kind of thing they teach you about up at the University. Breaking the nose of a recalcitrant pupil. No, sir, I don't recall as how any of my old professors lectured much on that." He laughed and slapped his knee.

John was a skinny fourteen-year-old, no taller than average. But listening to the way his teacher talked and laughed made him feel much bigger.

Mr. Crenshaw looked over and saw that John was not laughing or even smiling so he laughed again himself. "It's hard to believe, isn't it? Here I am out in Rock Springs after being in Chapel Hill not two months ago. You've heard of Chapel Hill, haven't you? I know you've heard of it, everyone's heard of it, but have you heard about it?"

He thought he saw John shrug so he said, "Oh, it's a marvelous place. When I first went up there from Lincolnton, I had heard it was wonderful—Daddy sent both of my older brothers there—but I had no idea how wonderful. Chapel Hill's an eye-opener, all right. You've heard of Franklin Street, haven't you?"

John had heard of a Franklin Boulevard down in Gastonia.

"Everybody should spend a day on Franklin Street before they die. Everybody.

"Of course, when I was an undergrad we still had Prohibition. Not that that stopped us, of course, merely made us more … clever." The teacher laughed again.

John measured Mr. Crenshaw. He was suddenly curious how Mr. Crenshaw would hold up in a fight against either of John's older brothers.

"Do you have any brothers?" Crenshaw asked. "I have two, both older. I think I mentioned them already."

He's not small, John thought, but not that big. His hands are smooth.

"They both went to the University, too. But they went on to law school. One's still there, the other's clerking for the circuit judge in Raleigh."

He seems nice, John thought. They'd kill him.

"I thought about going to law school. It's a noble profession. But, I came to realize that wasn't what I really wanted to do."

"You wanted to teach?" John asked doubtfully.

Crenshaw laughed. "No, no, not at all. Though it, too, is a noble profession. And I did think about continuing on at the University, studying for an advanced degree in English literature, maybe joining the faculty. But I realized I'm not truly a scholar, either."

Crenshaw smiled. "You'll never believe what I really want to do."

"What?"

"Write."

"Right?"

"Write. I hope to someday make my living as an author. I'm teaching here to earn some money, which I hope to save until I have enough to move to New York. Or possibly even Paris."

Crenshaw looked over at John, who was not looking at him.

"Mind you, teaching here in Rock Springs is helping me in more ways than just the saving of money. Being out here is—how to put it—watering my roots. Nurturing them. Helping me connect with and affirm the … essential … ruggedness … of my origins. That's something I can take with me to New York or Paris that's far more valuable than money."

The last few years had shown John that very little was more valuable than money. Money was freedom because money was power, and you didn't get either by breaking your back. Every one of his neighbors that lost a job, or lost a farm, lost power over himself and strength against others. Each summer day that John had spent dragging timber had buried powerfully within him the want to gamble his fortunes on possibilities. The way he heard men talked to by the men who signed their paychecks convinced him that he wanted nothing more than to sign his own paychecks.

John kept his face still as he turned over what Mr. Crenshaw had said. He liked that "essential ruggedness of my origins," that was good stuff. John measured Crenshaw again, wondering how much of him he could take.

"Just think," Crenshaw said, "perhaps someday your children's teacher will be teaching them my books." He laughed again.

Through the dust John saw Mundy's store and the road to his home. "You're gonna turn up here across from Mundy's," he said.

"Right up there at that store? You've been in that store?" Crenshaw had noticed that store several times, but had never quite felt like going in. The store was old and looked like it let out dark into the sunlight. Rough old men stood in its doorway in the morning and sat on its porch in the afternoon; wide working men and their trucks came and went all day. Crenshaw feared that his presence would somehow disturb the store's dirt.

John said he had been there, that he was in there all the time. Crenshaw smiled. "You feel like something to drink?"

"Sure."

"Why don't we stop in, then. I'm buying." The teacher pulled on the steering wheel and jerked the B-model Ford into the dry rutted red clay around the store. John listened to the shafts slowing as the valves and pistons stuttered to a stop. His eyes swept along the chassis and hood as he got out and walked up Mundy's front steps a pace behind his teacher.

Mr. Hager and Mr. Dellinger were sitting in the shade of the front porch, chewing tobacco and spitting over the railing. The teacher nodded to them, a bit too much John thought.

They nodded back and looked at John. "Hey there, young Gardiner."

"How y'all?"

"Fine, soon's the shade got here," Mr. Hager said.

"How's yours?" Mr. Dellinger asked.

"Fine, sir."

"You tell your paw bring that sawmill over my way next week."

"You wanting some timber cut?"

"Yeah, ain't no use leaving them woods standing by the creek bottom when I got bills to pay. You boys'll have to find another place for hunting."

"There's plenty of woods around. I'll tell him."

"Thank you, Johnny."

The teacher was waiting for him inside the door. "How y'all going to take a sawmill to somebody?"

"It sits on the back of a flatbed truck. We bolt it down and take it wherever the timber is."

"Oh. Oh, when you said your daddy owned a sawmill, I thought … Well, that's … downright … clever."

"Sure. My daddy's pretty smart."

His teacher let John walk ahead of him between copper line, small parts for tractor and truck engines, and barrels of sugar, flour, yeast and cornmeal. As they got near the counter at the back where Mundy sat and watched them, the teacher said to John, "You want a beer?"

Well, hell yes, John thought. I've never had me one of those.

"Sure," he said.

They walked clear of the aisle and the teacher leaned on the counter and held up two fingers and spoke to Mundy, who leaned and disappeared. John wasn't watching or listening, the prospect of beer at once overtaken. He walked carefully off to the side, toward the far corner. He didn't look when the teacher tapped him on the shoulder with the bottle, just took it and said, "Thank you." He walked closer to the corner.

The two sitting closest to him had their backs to him and sat hunched but wide-shouldered in their chairs, and for their shoulders John could only glimpse the faces of the men on the other side of the table. The hardwood creaked beneath him and the two closest looked quickly over their shoulders at him and he stopped until they looked back at their cards. Then he walked closer, until he could see the faces of the cards they held and the faces of the men they played.

John couldn't remember when he couldn't play cards. He couldn't remember how he had learned. His daddy didn't play cards, not even gin. Maybe one of his brothers had taught him, probably by taking in poker whatever robin's eggs or arrowheads he owned at the time, just like they taught him to swim by throwing him in the pond. For years he had watched the poker games in the corner of Mundy's, and when the men weren't at the table he and the other boys from the countryside sat and played for matchsticks or, in good times, pennies.

He used to know all the men who would sit around the table, and between hands John learned how men talk away from their families, and learned more and more about how much skill and how little luck was needed to win money gambling. But in the last year or so more strangers had come to play, and fewer east Lincoln County men, and gradually the men at the table became silent between hands.

"How's your beer?" the teacher asked behind him.

John looked at the bottle in his hand and took a gulp. The beer fizzed in his mouth and down his throat like Pepsi-Cola, but was dry and bitter and not at all sweet. He liked it.

"It's good beer. Thanks again," John said quietly.

"You're welcome. Thank you for taking care of that Abernathy boy," the teacher said, also quietly. He also watched the men at the table.

One of the men, sitting with his back in the corner, beside the rear door, had watched the teacher all the way from his B-model Ford, through the front door, up to the bar, and over to the table.

"You want in this game, friend?" he asked Crenshaw.

John wondered if Crenshaw had also heard the sneer in the man's voice. Crenshaw smiled slyly. "No, thank you. I'm fine just to watch a couple of hands, if y'all don't mind."

A man in a coat with no elbows glared. "I mind."

Crenshaw stared back and tried to think of something clever and disarming. The man in the corner said, "Aw, he's fine, Tully. Don't be so unneighborly. You got yourself an audience now." The rest of the men at the table laughed.

The man in the corner now looked at John. John had watched him while he had watched the teacher, and he didn't look away now.

The man took a coin from the pile in front of him and tossed it to John.

"One of them beers, son."

John tossed the coin back. "I ain't your son."

All the players put down their cards and looked at John. Crenshaw's head snapped sideways toward him. The man in the corner leaned back in his chair. "You ain't man enough to be smarting off to me, none, neither."

"I ain't smarting off. I ain't taking your orders, neither. I'm man enough to be asked."

Crenshaw's head snapped again, this time toward the man in the corner.

The man laughed. "Well, I'll be." He looked around the table with a smile. "Get a load of this little man."

"That boy's all right," one of the men said. "I know his daddy."

"His daddy ought to take a belt to him," the man in the corner said. "He's got a smart mouth. His daddy should've whupped it out him 'fore it gets him in trouble."

Crenshaw straightened where he stood and crossed his arms.

"You got something to say?" the man in the corner asked him.

Crenshaw breathed and smiled, and thought hard. "I don't suspect this young man needs anybody to talk for him."

"You don't?" The man in the corner shook his head. "I swear." He tossed the coin back to John. "If it ain't too much goddamn trouble, would you be so goddamn kind as to fetch me another goddamn beer?"

John took the coin to the counter and took the beer from Mundy. He brought it around the table and set it in front of the man in the corner. The man nodded.

Without a word John backed up and sat down on a high stack of wooden crates.

The man in the coat with no elbows twisted around and snarled and said, "Don't you be sitting behind me, kid," but another man said, "That boy's all right. That's King Gardiner's boy." Then another man said, "Which of King's boys are you?"

"John Gardiner."

The same man said, "Well, damn'd if you ain't gotten big. Ain't seen you in years."

The man in the corner set down his beer. "This is the first time I've ever played draw poker at a goddamn church social. Five more to you, Tully."

John watched Tully glare at his cards and saw him tap his ring finger on a fifty-cent piece before grabbing a five-dollar bill and throwing it into the pot. John saw the man to Tully's left raise his eyebrows a little before throwing in his five. He saw the man to his left, the man in the corner, do nothing but throw in a five and call. They all laid down their cards and the man in the corner raked in the pot.

Tully slammed his hands on the table. He scooped the small pile in front of him and counted quickly. The man who knew John nodded to the table and rose from his chair. He turned to John as he picked up his hat.

"Tell your daddy Pike Turbeyfield says hello."

"Yessir."

Turbeyfield nodded vaguely at Crenshaw and walked heavily across the hardwood, stopping at the counter to speak with Mundy.

Four dollars lay in the middle of the table, and four men stared at Tully. Tully stared into his cupped hands.

"You in, Tully?" the man in the corner asked.

"Tully," Turbeyfield called from the counter, "why don't you come on with me? I'll give you a ride."

"Tully ain't decided if he's in or not," the man in the corner said to Turbeyfield while staring at Tully.

"Tully," Turbeyfield said, almost softly, "come on now."

Crenshaw watched it all indistinctly, in a silent state of reception approaching adoration.

John listened to Tully breathe. Suddenly he saw Tully's eyes upon him, looking into his. John was surprised but he didn't show it; he watched Tully without turning away, wanting to know what that look in his eyes meant exactly, wanting to know what kind of man watched him now, somehow knowing that someday he would need to know.

Tully slowly lowered his eyes. He laid his money out on the table, picked out a dollar and threw it in.

"Tully," Turbeyfield said.

"Deal," the man in the corner ordered the man to his left, slapping the deck down on the table. The man shuffled them once and began to fling cards.

John heard a slow exhale and turned to see that now Turbeyfield was looking at him. He knew that look in Turbeyfield's eyes. He had seen his daddy look at one of his brothers like that, and he had once seen a preacher at the camp meeting look at all of them like that.

John could see a single bead of sweat slide down Tully's neck. He could see the man in the corner watch Tully, and watch John. John kept his face and eyes still.

The dealer flung fifth cards to the table and said, "Same as before, nothing wild, jacks or better."

They took their cards. The man to the dealer's left shook his head. "Pass," he said, and before he had finished hissing out the word Tully had snatched up a dollar. The silver piece hit the table before he had even said, "I'll open."

That's all wrong, John thought. Wait.

The man to Tully's left matched the dollar.

The man in the corner matched the dollar, then smiled and reached back into his pile. "How 'bout we see who the men are?" he asked as he threw in another dollar.

Four men blew through tight lips. The dealer drew two bills and laid them in slowly. The man to his left laid down his cards gently and leaned back. Tully snatched at a dollar and threw it in. The man to his left dropped his cards face down and shook his head.

"All right, then," the man in the corner said and grinned at Tully.

Tully took two cards and slapped them face down on the table.

What a slap, Crenshaw thought. What pain has gone into that slap, he asked himself.

John thought, three of a kind.

The dealer looked at Tully a moment, then drew two cards from the top of the deck and slid them across the table. Tully snatched them up, held them next to his other three, and became very still. He stared at his cards.

The man in the corner took a sip of beer and licked his lips. He looked at his cards carefully, thoughtfully, then picked out one and set it down on the table. "Just one," he told the dealer. Tully looked up at him.

Four of a kind, John thought, or he's drawing to a straight or a flush. Then he looked again at the man in the corner. No.

The dealer slid him his one card, then dropped three of his own and replaced them from the deck. He looked at Tully.

Tully was looking past the man in the corner through the window above him. He watched slow cars grow slowly up the state road, and he watched Mundy's shade oak shake in small winds. He saw the field beside Mundy's that ran empty this year, and he saw the woods beyond it.

"Your bet, Tully," the man in the corner said.

Tully put in a dollar.

"Afraid I'm going to have to raise you there," the man in the corner said. He threw in a five.

"I'm out," the dealer said without waiting.

Tully stared at his cards.

"That's four more to you, Tully," the man said. "I think you got that much. Maybe just that." He grinned.

From the way Tully held his cards John knew what he was about to do.

Don't, John thought. He's got nothing. You've got three at least. Don't.

"You didn't come here without enough cash, did you?" the man in the corner asked.

"Shut up, you," Turbeyfield yelled across the store. The man in the corner glared up at him, then turned back to Tully.

Don't, John thought.

"Come on now," the man in the corner said.

In a single motion Tully dropped his cards face down, scooped up what little was left of his money, rose from his chair and walked out of Mundy's store. John could hear movement all around the store that he hadn't heard a moment before. Turbeyfield glared at the man in the corner, raking in the pot, and followed Tully outside.

Crenshaw caught John's eye. He motioned to the door.

John watched the man in the corner stuff the money into his coat pockets, and caught the glint of gray steel from inside the coat. The man looked up at him and grinned.

"You want to try your luck—son?"

John stood up and walked out of Mundy's store. Not yet, he thought, you son-of-a-bitch.

The Donnoha Beast

Jamie Adams didn't like the way the sheriff smiled at them. All the men around the sheriff were smiling. Some of the country boys were, too. Jamie really didn't like that.

"You boys going to help us find this creature, huh?" the sheriff asked, still smiling.

Calvin spoke up first, of course. "Yes, sir. Why don't y'all just go on home?"

The big country boys sneered and cussed them. Calvin grinned back at them, deliciously. Woodrow locked eyes with the biggest, and cocked his head to one side. Jamie visibly tightened his grip on his .22 rifle. The country boys stopped slouching. It all happened and was done. The long sheriff loomed and spoke.

"Y'all ain't got much to worry about. Nobody's actually seen hide nor hair of that thing. Y'all'll shoot each other before you get a shot off at that creature."

Jamie looked around. A dozen men and boys looked to be there and about, and at his feet Jamie could see deep tire tracks trailing off into the darkness. They'd hurried out of football practice, changed clothes, grabbed their guns and hauled ass out here, but just couldn't make it from Ogburn Station to the county line before nightfall. The first story had been in the Sentinel the day before: two henhouses destroyed on a farm near Donnoha Bridge, nothing but feathers and blood found in the rubble. That morning the newspaper said a heifer's carcass had been found torn to pieces on a dairy farm; the sheriff had asked area hunters to join in the search for the unidentified predator. The paper called it the Donnoha Beast.

Whatever it is, that thing is probably long gone by now, Jamie thought.

"Whatever it is, that thing's probably long gone by now," the sheriff said.

"Y'all ain't even figured out what it is yet?" Calvin asked, still grinning.

The sheriff looked at him hard. Calvin still grinned, but Jamie saw him blink.

"I suspect it's just a panther come down from the mountains, following the river, looking for food. And it's probably moved right back up that river now. Got itself a couple of square meals and went on home.

"Course it might've stuck around. Lot easier to find food down here than up in the hills. Might not want to leave. Hope you boys know how to use them weapons."

A couple of the country boys snickered.

Calvin looked at Woodrow, then at Jamie.

"Might as well," Jamie said.

"I got a couple search parties out there already," the sheriff said. "Don't go shooting them, now."

One of the men standing by the sheriff pointed and said, "They's some tracks about a half-mile down the creek here. Last tracks we found. Y'all start there, if you can find it."

"Oh, we'll find it," Calvin said. "Don't expect that'll be any trouble." He let out a short, mean, high giggle, and led the other three down to the creek bank.

At creekside they were below the bottomland all around, and hidden in a track of hardwood from the farmland that ran to the river. Limbs laced from bank to bank, covering the scar of water run down from the near hills.

Sammy turned on his flashlight.

"How about those rednecks back there?" Calvin said.

"Fuckin' bumpkins," Woodrow said.

"Dumb country motherfuckers, ain't they?" Calvin asked nobody.

"Think they go to Northwest?" Sammy asked.

"Oh yeah. Couple of them looked familiar."

"When we play them this year?"

"End of October," Jamie said.

"Marking my calendar," Woodrow said.

"Oh, hell yeah," said Calvin. "Gonna spend some extra time sharpening up my spikes. That one might even be a knuckler."

For some games Calvin tucked a pair of brass knuckles into his waistband. On the first series he lined up for, he'd slip them on, show them to the man across, and say, "You ain't coming this way, are you?"

"Shit, Calvin, like you wouldn't've needed the knuckles for the Northwest game anyway," Woodrow said, since only he could.

"If the sheriff hadn't been standing there, we'd've kicked their country asses back there," Sammy said.

"We?" Calvin asked him.

"Yeah," Sammy said. "We could've took 'em."

"I'mona ask you again," Calvin said, grinning in the dark. "We?"

Woodrow and Jamie could see where Calvin was going. Maybe Sammy can too, Jamie thought, and he don't need that now.

"Wonder how those boys get along with all those country club kids that go to Northwest," Jamie said.

"Bet they're best friends," Calvin said, pissed that Jamie was changing the subject. "Bet they swap spit in the showers."

"They ought to be best friends," Jamie said. "That's why they always got the good teams. You got the rich kids bringing in all that money for the best equipment, and them big hosses from the country winning the games."

"Yeah."

"Yeah."

Even as he finished his sentence Jamie knew it wasn't entirely true. But for now he liked the way it sounded.

"I don't know," Calvin said. "You have to watch out for those rich boys. They can be dangerous. Ain't that right, Sammy?"

"Huh?"

"Sammy knows how dangerous those rich boys can be." Calvin laughed. "Or, if he don't, Wanda does."

"Shut up, Calvin," Sammy said without looking at him.

Woodrow said, "She done you wrong, bud," trying to be sympathetic. That was as close as he could get.

Jamie looked away. He looked down the creek, closely along both sides, trying to figure where the tracks might be.

Calvin punched him in the shoulder. "The course of true love," he said, "did never run smooth." Calvin punched him again. "That's good, ain't it? Ain't that right?"

Jamie saw Sammy glare at Calvin for a moment, then glare at the ground in front of him. He's almost angry enough, Jamie thought; they don't even know what he's got in mind. He won't try anything with Calvin, though. He'd fight Woodrow before he'd fight Calvin. Woodrow'd knock him down quick, and then it'd be over. Calvin would knock him down slow, and then there'd be no telling what he'd do.

Jamie couldn't see very far in front of himself, so he listened, and watched the ground at his feet. Creatures were moving unseen on all sides, freezing as the boys approached, breaking as they neared and passed. The hardwood brush crackled.

Jamie stopped.

"Oh, shit," he said, and the others stopped. Jamie nodded at his feet.

The tracks were damaged and huge. Footprints littered the clearing and smashed the clean lines of the searched-for paws. That left only vague impressions, partial prints the imagination filled in. But on the edge of the bank, dug deep into the mud, where anything large would have to brace itself to drink … Those claws had to be three inches long.

The dry limbs above them rattled. Something slapped the mud on the other side. The underbrush uphill cracked against some moving weight.

"Can't really tell where the tracks lead off to," Calvin said.

"Not even which direction," he added.

"No," Jamie said.

"Damn," Sammy said.

"Yeah," Jamie said.

"It probably kept moving this way," Woodrow said as he pointed with the rifle barrel. "Back toward the river. There's good cover all along here. Real good cover."

"Yeah," Jamie and Calvin both said.

"Probably moved uphill, where it can watch what goes by along the creek."

"Yeah."

"Probably."

They drove fast the length of Old Town Road.

"Damn," Sammy said, "I thought Coach was gonna rip Caudle's head off in practice today."

"Coach should rip Caudle's head off," Calvin said. "The fuck-up. When's he planning on getting that play right, baseball season?"

"Pretty boy," Woodrow said.

"That's our problem," Calvin said. "We got a damn pretty boy playing halfback."

"Yeah," Sammy said, "we need us a damn hoss in the backfield, 'stead of a lard-ass like Henry and a pretty-boy like Caudle. Need us a stud."

"Yeah, a stud, huh, Sammy," Calvin said. "Like you? Huh? A stud like you?"

Sammy spat.

"That must be why Wanda dumped you to go out with that rich boy from Reynolds, huh?" Calvin grinned at Woodrow and Jamie. "Sammy was too much of a stud for her."

"Shut up, Calvin," Sammy said, but he let his voice rise.

"Uh-oh. Don't get mad, now," Calvin teased. But Woodrow and Jamie weren't laughing, so Calvin told Sammy he was just picking and changed the subject back to football. The four of them had figured out how to get their team to the state championship by the time Calvin pulled off Indian Avenue and pulled up in front of Sammy's house.

"Thanks" was all Sammy said as he climbed out of the backseat.

"See y'all tomorrow," Jamie said as he opened his door.

"What, you getting out here?" Calvin asked.

"Yeah."

"You ain't going out to the Shack with us?"

"Nah. I'm gonna stay here a while."

Calvin looked at him, a suspicion bouncing along his eyes and brows while Jamie stared back. Finally he grinned, taunted, and said so long, boys. Woodrow nodded as they pulled out.

"Thanks, Jamie," Sammy said.

"Sure."

"No, I really appreciate you doing this."

"Sure."

"We better get going."

Jamie lived three blocks away. Sammy drove him in his dad's Ford and let him out at the curb.

"So I'll meet you down at the restaurant?"

"Yeah," Jamie said.

"The Smokehouse up at Thruway?"

"Yeah, I know."

"You want me to wait on you?"

"No. I'll be there."

"All right. I really appreciate it, Jamie."

"Don't worry about it."

"All right."

Lights were on throughout Jamie's house, in his sister's room, the living room, the kitchen. He walked in and could hear his mother washing dishes. His father was reading the paper in his chair in the living room, while the baby played with a fire truck at his feet.

"That unloaded?" his father asked, without looking up.

"Yes, sir." He'd unloaded the rifle in the driveway, and he held out the rounds in his hands.

"You get it, Grizzly?"

"No. Never even saw it. It's probably long gone by now." Jamie replaced the .22 in the closet. "Did see its tracks, though."

"Really?"

"It's a big'un, whatever it is."

"Really."

The baby tottered to Jamie's legs and grabbed hold.

"Hey there, sport," Jamie said.

"Hey." The baby smiled.

"How you been, tough guy?"

"Fun."

"I bet so." Jamie pretended to punch him in the belly. The baby squealed and laughed, and slapped Jamie on the thigh.

"How was practice?" his father asked.

Jamie shrugged. "Fine."

"Y'all be ready for Hanes this Friday?"

"I guess."

"What's this guessing? You best know."

"Yes, sir. I will by Friday." Jamie patted the baby on the head, and he tottered off. "Who you going to root for?"

"I'm going to root for Hanes to win and you to play well."

"You ain't going to root for us?"

"I'm going to root for you."

"Can't root against your old school, huh?"

"I could. I just don't want to." His father turned the page.

Jamie smiled. "I'm going back out with Sammy."

His father glanced at the clock. "Don't y'all be out too late."

"I won't."

"And don't y'all be getting into trouble."

"No, sir."

"All right. Speak to your mother on your way out."

"Yes, sir."

Jamie did speak to her, quickly and without stopping. If he stopped to let her talk he'd have to work hard to leave. As she scrubbed the pot he could smell the vinegar in which she'd cooked the collard greens he'd missed.

Their street ran along the spine of a hill, rising up out of the hollow where the mineral springs had bubbled up. Jamie drove up the street slowly. He drove past the small houses and square lots, the puny and binding homesteads their fathers, veterans of the war and not long down from the hills, had worked for like dogs. He drove away from the little colony of what their parents had hoped would be a gentler life. Jamie thought of football, of the movement of players on the field, until he reached the restaurant.

"Wanda told me he's taking her here." Sammy leaned on the door of Jamie's car, smoking, bouncing and looking around. "I figure we'll wait here for them to come out, then follow them a ways."

"Why didn't you get Woodrow to do this?" Jamie asked. "He's top fist. The whole damn county's scared of him."

"I don't want this cocksucker scared of Woodrow, I want him scared of me."

"Oh, he ain't gonna be scared of me?"

"Dammit, Adams, you know what I mean. Besides, I just … I don't know. Hell, you don't even have to get out of your car, just block him in for me."

"That's exactly what I'll do," Jamie said, irritated. "The rest of this is up to you."

"That's just fine. That's the way I want it. I can take care of this. This is something I've got to do. I've got to show Wanda she can't treat me like this. Show this rich boy motherfucker, too. Not going to take this shit."

Jamie nodded. "You best go wait in your car. Be ready. I'll follow you." He was starting to wonder if Sammy was going to shut up. He'd keep talking and not even notice them leaving.

If he wasn't actually talking to him, Jamie felt sorry for Sammy. He was an all right guy, he just wasn't as all right as the rest of the guys they ran with. When he was talking to Sammy, though, or when Sammy was talking to him, Jamie just got mad.

Jamie hoped Sammy actually was capable of beating up this Reynolds boy. He figured he was. Sammy was at least tough enough to run with him and Woodrow and Calvin, even if they always gave him shit, so probably he was tough enough to handle this.

Jamie saw Wanda before Sammy did. But Sammy saw her soon after, and started his car before her date's Buick had left the parking lot. Jamie followed Sammy out, and the three cars drove off in an unbalanced line.

Soon they were driving down a dark and empty street, with a few fine homes set far back from the curb. Jamie watched Sammy's Ford pull away from his Chevy.

Lot of woods on this road, Jamie thought, and not many cars.

Sammy tagged the Buick's rear bumper; the Buick lurched and shuddered and Jamie could hear the Reynolds boy yell. Sammy was already in the oncoming lane, shooting around the Buick, then went sideways in front of it and all their brakes screamed.

The Buick's dome light came on. Jamie saw the Reynolds boy, his hand on Wanda's hand. She was trying to hold him inside the car. He pushed her hand off, said something to her, and tried to look like he was in control. Maybe he thinks he is, Jamie thought.

But when the boy stepped out of his car he finally recognized the presence of Jamie's car behind him. He stared at Jamie's windshield as the idea of danger reached him. By then Sammy was on him, and had swung once. The Reynolds boy clutched his face and fell.

Sammy can't hit that hard, was Jamie's first thought. Then his mind caught up with his eyes and he saw that something had been in Sammy's hand.

Sammy grabbed the boy by the V-neck of his sweater and pulled him up and pushed him against the Buick. He stuck the pistol between the boy's eyes and Jamie was out of his car.

"What the hell are you doing?" Jamie screamed. His voice was high. Wanda had been screaming, but had stopped. She was cussing Sammy.

"Goddamn you, Sammy, don't. Oh my God, Sammy, don't. Goddamn you Sammy. Goddamn you."

"What the hell is this?" Jamie yelled.

"You can drive on now," Sammy said.

"What the hell are you thinking?"

"Why don't you just go on now."

Jamie was calm. Suddenly Jamie realized he had become extremely calm. He was almost numb. He felt like a powerful machine in neutral, like a fast car idling.

"Sammy, you do not want to do this." He had no idea where Sammy had gotten the pistol, and he truly did not care. "Sammy, you know this ain't the thing to do."

Jamie felt as if his power was immense. Now the whole world seemed calm to him: the boy, Wanda, the road, the trees, the three humming engines in the moon's false and incomplete light. The world seemed as solid and undisturbable as his words.

"Put the gun down, Sammy."

"Put that gun down, Sammy."

Without doubt he watched Sammy put his thumb on the hammer and lower it slowly to the pin. He watched Sammy lower his arm and the gun and stuff it into his waistband. The stone face of the world collapsed in a rolling, dusty heap, and Jamie felt his legs almost give.

Sammy smacked the Reynolds boy in his already-bleeding face. The boy winced and cowered, and Sammy punched him in the stomach to send him back to the ground.

"You better be fucking grateful to my friend, asshole. And you best leave my girl alone."

Wanda dove and crawled across the front seat, and Jamie noticed she wasn't crying. "I ain't your girl no more," she screamed as she reached for her date.

"Don't you see now, Wanda," Sammy pleaded. "Don't you see? Don't you …"

"Get the hell out of here," Jamie yelled, his calm gone, his voice high, his hands shaking and his legs now twitching to run. "Get out of here! Go home!"

Sammy turned and walked, then ran, to his car. He straightened the car in a two-point turn and was gone.

Jamie was somehow back in his own car. Wanda was helping her date into the Buick as he drove past. She stared at his windows. She did not look grateful.

Squirrel Hunting

Billy Adams, a rifle resting in each small hand, looked nervously at his grandfather, who pulled the big Jeep to the side of the road. An old man walked towards them through the grass on the shoulder.

"I didn't think it was safe to pick up hitchhikers," Billy leaned and whispered.

"I think we can handle this one."

The old man opened the door behind Billy and climbed in. "I thank you, sir. My car broke down a ways back, and I got to go home and get some parts."

"That must've been your car we passed a few miles back. Blue Oldsmobile?"

"That's her."

"How far to your house?"

"Just up this road a piece."

"Well, we'll be happy to give you a ride," Billy's grandfather said as he pulled back onto the road. "John Gardiner."

"Pleased to meet you, Mr. Gardiner. Vance Simms."

Vance Simms leaned toward the middle to look at Billy.

"How are you, young man?"

"Fine. Sir."

"Good. And what's your name?"

"Um, Billy."

"Y'all doing some hunting?"

"Yeah," Gardiner said. "We're going to do a little squirrel hunting."

"Uh-hah. I bet you like squirrel huntin', don't you, Billy?"

"Um, this is my first time."

"Really? How old are you?"

"Eleven. Sir."

"Oh. Well, I bet you'll get you some nice ones. Got to look sharp, though, them squirrels is fast. You a good shot?"

"I'm okay."

"I bet you are." Vance Simms sat back and looked around. "You one of the Gardiners from out this way?"

"I am. I grew up out here."

"But you don't live here now?"

"No, I worked in Charlotte for thirty years. I'm retired now, live over on the lake."

Vance Simms nodded and turned his head to the window. The jeep curved and dashed by the pines and the sweetgums and the bare, iron-red soil. Billy stared out his window and held the rifles tightly.

"You work in town?" Gardiner asked.

"No, I got me a little farm. Grow tobacco."

"That's something. Not many of y'all left."

"That's the truth. Keeps getting harder and harder just to run your own little plot and," and even Billy could hear his voice trail off.

John Gardiner nodded.

The road sloped down into a hollow. The insides of graying barns and curing sheds could be seen where the boards had rotted and fallen. The hard clay shone on the side of the road, rubbed raw by the erosion of the rain gulleys.

"You can drop me off right up here, sir," Simms said. "That there's my drive."

"I'll take you on up to your house."

"No, I can make it fine myself. It ain't far."

"You got a way back to your car?"

"Oh yeah. Yeah, I got a way."

"All right."

Billy's grandfather slowed down and pulled over next to a dirt-and-gravel road with a line of silver mailboxes at the head of it. The old man opened the door, but didn't climb out.

"I'd appreciate it if you'd let me pay you for your trouble."

"No, you don't need to do that. This wasn't any trouble." "All right, sir, if you say so. I am much obliged to you."

Billy's grandfather turned around and put out his hand. "No trouble at all."

"Y'all have some good hunting, now. Bye-bye, Billy." He shook Gardiner's hand and slapped Billy's bony shoulder.

The door slammed shut, and the Jeep climbed Gardiner Road up the ridge.

"Now, when you start driving in a few years you don't need to be picking up hitchhikers. Too many crazies out there. Didn't used to be like that."

"Yeah, that's something that people talk a lot about on TV, that you shouldn't hitchhike or pick up anybody, 'cause you never know who might be like a criminal or something."

"Well, I figured that was his car broke down back there. And he didn't look much like a criminal. And, besides, we have the guns."

Billy looked down his .22, from barrel to butt, very seriously. "Didn't you hitchhike all the way across the country?"

" I did."

"Mom told me."

"The day after I graduated from high school, my parents took me up to that crossroads we passed a while ago and dropped me off. I wanted to go out to California."

"Why?"

"I wanted to work on airplanes. That's where the airplanes were built."

"I want to hitchhike like that someday."

"The world's a different place now. It wouldn't be safe for you to do that."

"What about when I'm eighteen?"

"No, not even when you're eighteen."

Billy knew his grandfather had hitched across the country, and he knew his father had hitchhiked all the time when he was a teenager and didn't have a car. He knew both his father and grandfather had served in the military, and both were very good shots. He knew both men were very good and successful businessmen.

They turned off Gardiner Road, onto a private drive. When they came alongside a brown barn they stopped.

"Hand me my rifle and that box of shells." Billy passed the rifle in his left hand, making sure to keep the barrel up, and then reached down for a box of .22 shells. He liked how the box felt heavy in his hand.

They walked through mud toward the barn. Billy liked the solid trump of the hiking boots that his father had bought a few months ago when Billy joined the Boy Scouts. He held the rifle carefully and closely, breathing in the disturbing smell of gun oil and the smoky taint of past firings. He was getting used to these smells, and starting to like them. Horses snorted at them over a barbed-wire fence.

Then Billy heard the clink of dog tags behind him and he had to stiffen. He looked quickly, and a hound was running slowly at them from across the road. Billy kept walking, tightly, afraid and ashamed and aware. He could make himself breathe slowly, but his ears twitched and pulled themselves up and back, tightening the skin over his temples. The skin tightened and drew taut the scars beside his left eye.

He could make himself keep walking, and he could make himself not think about the long-gone dog that had knocked him down, clawed and bit. He could not make himself not be afraid. He waited for this dog to jump, and he breathed, and he hoped he wouldn't scream. He hoped he would someday no longer be afraid of all the things he was afraid of now, because fighting all those fears was making him very tired.

His grandfather appeared not to notice the dog. He handed his rifle to Billy, opened the gate between the barn and the fence, held it for Billy and the hound to slip through, and then swung it shut. The horses trotted closer, sniffing and snorting, and one put his muzzle nearly into Billy's face. With his hands full of rifle and his back against the fence, Billy could only lean away. The horse leaned in closer. The horses and the dog did not bother each other. The dog kept his distance from the horses.

Billy started glancing at the dog as they walked through the field. His coat was mud brown. He moved slowly, kept his head down, and didn't bark.

Billy looked up at his grandfather's back. "Pappy, this is the best-behaved dog I've ever seen. I mean, it hasn't, like, tried to jump on me or lick me or anything."

His grandfather looked at the hound for the first time that day.

"Did you notice that dog only has three legs?"

Billy looked again as the dog hobbled away. The left hind leg ended at the knee; the dog's thigh was thin and drawn up against his side, and the skin was stretched tight over the bone. The other hind leg moved in jerks to keep up.

"Oh. No. I hadn't seen …"

"Uh-huh."

They did not speak again while they hunted. They stepped over and through the low brambled brush that bordered the woods. Billy could hear, and then see, squirrels rushing among the bared branches that struck out over him. He could hear the songs and see the flights of jays, crows, cardinals, and robins. He slipped the safety off and chambered a round when his grandfather motioned him to, and they walked deeper into the forest. Billy waited for further permission to fire. The dog stayed behind, wandering away from them and from the horses in the field.

Symbolon

I don't know how long I lay there, breathing hard, but I don't think it was very long. I stared at the ceiling until I could see its patterns in the dark. I remembered that my daughter had climbed into bed with us earlier in the night, and I made sure that I had struck neither her nor her mother. They slept soundly; my daughter had wrapped her hand in her mother's hair.

I was surprised to have dreamt such a fantastic dream, such a potent and mythic narrative. I remembered the dream, and I decided to try to remember it. I was disturbed and challenged by what I remembered. I would search the dream for meanings and secrets; my dreams so rarely told me anything. I got up to use the bathroom.

Most of my dreams were so unimaginative they could easily have happened in real life. At the worst times of my life—when my parents died, when my daughter had her tonsils out—my dreams were always commonplace. When things were fine I dreamed of fights and falling.

Relieved, I went back to my bedroom. My wife and child had spread across the mattress, taking my place to lay down. I stood there, watching them breathe, unaware, protected from the battles and hardships of the world by the work that filled my waking hours, by the sacrifices I had made, by the identities that I had given up. Suddenly and unreasonably angry, I looked across their bodies to the window, looking through my reflection to my yard and the shadow of the woods behind it. I breathed deeply and felt ashamed.

I decided to go ahead and shave, and shower, and dress myself for work. I dreaded my first appointment of the morning, so I decided to be at the office early, to greet that meeting with a bit of momentum. Before I left I wrote a brief note for my wife, set it on our bedside table, and kissed both her and our daughter very, very lightly.

From my office window I could watch the sunrise over campus, over the magnolias and the neoclassical lines of the dormitories. Remembering my dream, I reflected that I lived in a city that was, in geography, in history, and in spirit, as far as one could be from New Orleans and still be in the South. My city was not at the mouth of a mighty river, strategically crucial and assured of riches. Two Indian trading paths had once crossed here; a Calvinist Scot had opened a trading post. Commerce and industry had built this city where nature had no need of one. Commerce and industry were building a whole new South. Yet another letter sat on my desk, asking me to take a leading part in this project of a new South, asking me to leave my position at the college to enter those wars. On my desk was yet another letter from Robert Lee McLeod.

Through church I knew, liked, and was liked by Bob McLeod, who was then an executive vice president. We had gotten to know one another better while working together on the mayor's Congressional run. Bob described his bank as a place of energy, of intellectual challenge.

"It's not about the numbers anymore," Bob said to me at lunch one day. "The numbers are there. The Sun Belt's exploding. Now it's about the direction that those numbers are going to take.

"We play the game to win," he said. "That's a given on our team. The question, then, is what game are we going to play? Are we going to be satisfied being the number one bank in the state, in the South, or in the nation?

"Look," he said, "it's been almost one hundred years since the end of Reconstruction, but if we need coverage to make a deal happen, we still have to go hat-in-hand to the big boys in New York. Long-term, that's unacceptable. I-95 runs both ways. We win when we're a major player on the world stage, if we have to drag this city kicking and screaming behind us."

Of course I would leave the college to work for him. I would gladly exchange towers of ivory for towers of steel. I was not content as an associate dean. I knew I would someday soon be dean, and someday probably provost, and someday possibly president of this college or another, but I did not see myself content in any of those roles, either. Like most men of my time, place, and station, I had grown up on stories of generals, of Robert E. Lee in particular; as a boy my career goal was war hero. In prep school, Lee's idolization of Washington had led me to the lives of the founders. Once I was in college at the Citadel, the study of Washington led me to the noble Greeks and Romans. Strong interest in the classics, in Plutarch and in Pericles, had carried me into academia, but I never thought of classical studies as an academic exercise. I was truly in pursuit of the good. I had always wanted to know how to engage the world with honor. I enjoyed my studies and I enjoyed administration, but here at last was a war to fight, a noble war to be won with banknotes rather than bombs.

The sun was above the dormitories. I could hear heels clicking down the marble halls of the administration building, and I could see students passing on the quad outside my window. I had half an hour until my first appointment. I walked down to the cafeteria for a late breakfast.

The cafeteria was crowded in the morning, the only time of day in which students would rather take their meals here than off campus. I nodded or spoke to the several I knew, those who had taken my course on the rhetoric of the Roman Republic, those who had been in my office for a grievance or for discipline. They smiled or said hello or ignored me. They went on about their transactions, presented meal cards for their food, maneuvered to make their place more central within the tables of their friends. By every pair of feet a stack of books rested on the tile. Fine students attended our school, fine children of the South, who would almost all proceed to lives of accomplishment and contribution. If their conversations now were loud and hardly worthy of the name conversation, if their minds were fixed on parties and the opposite sex, so be it—a reflection, to my mind, of vitality. For four years they were right to act silly, to be cocksure and shallow, as students had been since the youth of Saint Augustine, at least. I had faith that we would leave something inside them that would serve them in good stead. Part of our job, I thought, should be the encouragement of a certain assurance—an assurance of ability and station, a confidence in the role, the status, the usefulness that they would take up after graduation. I cherished those who displayed a classical restraint, who possessed already a moral seriousness, but I cherished them in part because I worried for their futures. Such a one who reached the mean and reached it with grace was to be doubly beloved.

I watched her walk in. She walked with the kind of balance and reserve that shows why we give our daughters training in dance. Fair and open was the countenance of her face; her aspect and her lines achieved the same balance as her stride. She was a classical studies major; she had enrolled in my class after her year of study in the Mediterranean. She was from an old Alabama family, the baby of a clan that had fought Creeks for a frontier, the daughter of a captain of the steel industry. I felt the dread rise in my throat as she walked along the far wall, spoke greeting to a tableful of her friends, and then saw me. She smiled shyly across the cafeteria and sat with her back to the wall.

This is why I am frantic for dreams. I courted and married my wife while I worked toward my doctorate. I studied at a great university in one of the great cities of the Northeast. My wife was and is a charming lady, good-hearted, elegant and refined, delightful in her wit. Her father was a small-town doctor, avuncular and knowing; he had sent his only daughter north to study music. I knew soon after I met her that she would be the love of my life, the proper companion and helper to my plans and goals. I failed her not long before our wedding.

For a year I had worked in the Classics department with a woman who was striking and brilliant and stirring. She was an expert on the odes of Horace. She was half-French and passionate, several years older than myself, and her name was Isabel. I thought our flirtation was harmless. I thought I might need one last fling, before I stood at the altar to swear my faith before God and man. Perhaps that is what I thought. Perhaps I thought I needed to learn something, a thing learned best with a woman who boasted of having made love in the shadow of Notre Dame, best learned luxuriously in a bed in a city so stratified and dense that each block, each brownstone held civilizations unknown. I did not give in to lust. I pursued the measure this woman had achieved. She was a phenomenal creature. After 28 days our senses of honor insisted that it end; her sense of honor insisted she inform my fiancee.

I called her a liar, publicly and privately, to others and, soon, to myself. The woman was known to be manic and unstable, and her word was overmatched against mine. My fiancee, my colleagues, my professors all believed me. The woman left the university and the city, and we heard unfounded rumors. I thought such talk was irresponsible.

A few years later, when my wife and I first tried to start a family, I found myself unable not to think of Aeschylus and fate. I tortured myself with the idea of a vengeful God, of Furies who would demand satisfaction. I considered a confession, but was unwilling to lay such a pain on my wife. I prayed for dreams that would wake me well before dawn, that I might sit in the dark and make interpretations. For such a dream, and for someone else's telling of that dream, Agamemnon sacrificed his own beloved child to secure a good wind. For nine months I slept soundly and remembered nothing in the morning. I steeled myself for retribution. I steeled myself for stillbirth, or, worse, deformity, a child born incomplete. My daughter, when born, was perfect.

Virginia Roe was on time for her appointment. She drew breath to speak. She had been raised to speak properly in a soft and patient voice. I was happy to listen.

"My father found out about us," she said. "He intends to tell the president."

I exhaled more loudly than I meant to.

"I don't want my father to do that. I don't want him to be fired. What he did was wrong—he lied to me. He lied about his wife and children. But I take responsibility for my part in this. I am not a child. I'm sorry to trouble you with this, but I did not know who else to turn to.

"I've always admired your integrity," she said.

I do not remember what words I said to her. I hated to tell her that their affair had been widely known for some time, and that just as well known was that this was not the first time he or she had done such a thing. And so I did not. I recoiled at the thought of such a man possessing such a creature as her. For a year now I had watched him swagger through campus, playing to the hilt the outsider role his writer-in-residency gave him, and I regretted allowing his hiring. Her effort at composure was apparent. She must have cried over this before now, and more than once. I told her I could take care of the situation.

"He gave me this," she said, and held out a symbolon, half of a small tablet, no larger than a coin, with a scroll printed across its face. An ancient and honored token of another's role in one's own fulfillment, made complete when connected to the half held by your beloved. "Could you please give it back to him?"

I told her I would be sure to do so.

In my dream there was a girl, and so there had to be a villain. They did not appear or arrive; I did. I appeared where I had been all along, and they were wholly formed and known to me, without relations or progressions for me to figure out.

The villain wanted the girl, of course, but he also wanted me. He could create, he was creating, gray soulless creatures out of those who had once had will. He had a gang of them, drained and impervious, and soon he would have an army. The girl was somehow key to the gathering of this army, and I was somehow crucial to her.

We were upstairs in an old mansion in a town like New Orleans, but on a street like those in the Garden District, not like those in the French Quarter. Pleasant trees, stirred by a comfortable breeze, lined the broad street platted by young Americans, where they had built stately homes upriver from the miasma. We were trapped in the corner of the house, in a pre-Raphaelite bedroom of intricate patterns and heavy air, a room that had climbed its way out of the wrecks of the Reconstruction, a room that held the best of the mercantile South. The girl stood behind me; the villain attacked, reaching with his hand and conjuring with his eyes. I could feel my will slipping from me; I could feel my attention going dull. I could feel my soul's exit like an exhalation, like a relief, and I had no sense that I dreamed. Startled, I drew breath and drew my soul back in. Music played - had been playing - I could hear music playing outside on the street. A brass band passed at the head of a parade. Below on the street was abandon. I marshalled my will and focused on the villain.

I saw him then as the Devil he was; I saw him then as Lucifer. He had only appeared as a grave and accomplished man because he knew what I wanted so well. I broke from his stare and saw myself in a mirror. I leaned into the mirror, looking closely at my eyes, and I could see the ashen scars of my near defeat. They followed the paths of my veins, creeping snakelike from the white of my eye into the iris, and if I'd let them grow a moment more they'd have blinded me. I stared longer, horrified, looking for the messy blush of a soul. Instead I saw the mud and blood of a wolf in the rings around my eyes.

Lucifer leaned behind me, his reflection plain to see, and if his breath was foul I did not notice. He spoke softly in my ear of his coming triumph, in arcane words I recognized. I tried to remember them. I only remembered his last sentences: "You shouldn't be surprised. There's more than you would think. It beats with the heart of every man." I turned to face him.

He tried to strike but I caught his hand. He laughed in his strength but I, at last, was formidable. I twisted his hand and wrist until the muscles pulled off the bone, but he could stand the pain. He struck me with his other fist, and I struck him with mine, but neither of us could summon any force. I realized I could only win this fight with more unnatural twisting. I wrenched his arm, bending his hand until it bent beneath his wrist. He screamed. He pulled away from me, shocked but not yet defeated. I faced the Devil with equal strength.

So when the girl, still behind me, put her hand on my shoulder and whispered soft words in my ear, I felt a burrowed fear explode inside me. I could feel my stomach and lungs and heart contract, all wanting to stop, and I woke up.

The Battler

Beth Adams watched her son through the window in the kitchen door, and wondered how he and his father could do this to her. She watched Billy kick at rocks and weeds in the vacant lot next door. She could see that his hands were shaking. He picked up a dirt clod, threw it, and watched it fly into the woods behind the lots on their side of the cul-de-sac. A line of trees, ten yards deep, ran east from behind their yard all the way to Waverly Road. Those woods screened Chelsea Drive from the creek and the mile-wide tobacco field on the other side. Their house was on the far end of Chelsea Drive, where houses were not much older than Beth's daughter Maggie, and she was only two. Behind their yard the thin screen became a pine forest that spread west, uninterrupted until it was cut by the highway into Raleigh. When they'd moved in last summer, Billy and his brother Luke had explored the woods with toy guns and remnants of their father's Marine uniform. They'd met other boys, made friends and enemies, and stopped missing Winston-Salem quite as fiercely. In the fall, though, one of the neighbors had spied a man dressed in a flimsy shirt and tattered pants, leaning against a pine, watching the yards and houses. Jim Adams and Wayne Gibson next door had gone into the woods after him, but the man heard them and ran away. All the kids in the subdivision had been barred from the woods after that.

Billy was looking into the woods where he had thrown the dirt clod. Beth wondered how far he could see without his glasses.

A boy Billy's age walked up Chelsea Drive towards him. Beth guessed that this was Brian. She breathed deeply. Brian and Billy stood face to face, but all they did was talk. They didn't seem to be angry. Brian had his hands in his pockets. She could see them shaking hands, could see Billy walking inside. Beth could see it, and she watched and waited for it to happen.

Behind her Maggie screamed in a way Beth recognized. "Luke," Beth shouted, "leave your sister alone." Luke came running, hopping, smiling, out of the den and through the kitchen. He stopped at the island counter, a good six feet from Beth, and slid in his socks to her side.

"Has it started?" He stood on his toes and peered through the window.

Beth was about to say, "No, and I don't think it's going to." She had turned so she could look at Luke when she said this. But as she opened her mouth she heard a shout outside. Another boy, the same age as Billy and Brian, was pedalling his bike up the street as hard as he could. He was calling out. Three more boys came across the yards on the other side of the street. Two more boys rode up on bicycles. They surrounded Billy and Brian, and they were happy.

At her last bridge club before they left Winston-Salem, a friend had warned Beth that these small towns east of Raleigh were closed-off and cliquish. So far, though, Beth had found this town no worse than Winston-Salem, with its old money and all its heirs of the righteous congregation who'd founded the town as their red-brick haven on a hill. Here, the plant Jim ran was a major employer, and the Chamber of Commerce sought him out. The only ones who felt excluded were her boys. She had expected that for Billy, God bless him, but Luke—something had to be wrong with anyone, other than his little sister, who didn't like Luke.

Beth saw Brian look at Billy and shrug. Then he hit Billy hard in the jaw.

Brian swung again but Billy leaned and slipped his punch. He stuck his left fist flush into Brian's face. He swung his right fist and hit Brian on the side of the head. Brian stumbled backwards and dropped his hands. Billy chased him, throwing both fists as hard and as fast as he could, one after the other.

Beth felt a flush in her throat and in her face. Later she understood the flush was one of pride: in her son, and in her husband, for teaching her son well.

But Billy wasn't strong enough to knock Brian down, and he wasn't mean enough to keep hitting once he saw that Brian couldn't or wouldn't hit back anymore. Billy stepped back and held his fists in front of his face like a tiny, bony boxer.

Brian lunged, swinging wildly. Billy ducked and Brian ran past him, but he reached out and got his arm around Billy's throat. Brian turned and clung to Billy, turning and pulling and squeezing until he had Billy trapped in a chokehold.

Beth watched Billy's face twist in pain and panic and she reached to open the door, but Luke was in her way, bouncing on his feet and yelling.

"He's going to do it! He's going to! Do it, Billy!"

Beth knew what Luke was talking about. Every time her boys wrestled with their father, Jim did it to them, and he told them and showed them how it was done. Beth's mother-in-law was a nervous woman, but she never minded her sons moving back the furniture to wrestle. Neither did Beth. She trusted Jim's strength to keep her boys from getting hurt, and she understood their need to roughhouse, and in a way she was glad for it.

Billy leaned back into Brian. He shoved his elbow into Brian's gut. He grabbed the arm around his neck and pried it loose. He reached back with his right hand and grabbed the back of Brian's neck. He lowered his right shoulder and pulled with his right arm, and Brian fell over him and laid down hard on the ground, flat on his back. Billy knelt over him and held him down and punched him in the face, twice, three times, four, five, again, again. Beth pushed Luke aside and opened the kitchen door.

"You boys stop that! Billy Adams, you get in here right this minute!"

Billy stood and walked across the lot. The circle of boys scattered.

Brian rolled over onto his hands and knees, knelt, stood, and walked away alone.

Luke was jumping, laughing, yelling, throwing wide punches in the air.

"Are you all right?" Beth asked when she'd shut the door behind Billy. "Does it hurt anywhere?"

"Not right now." Billy's face was red, with spots that were redder than others. He was breathing hard and trying to get past them.

"Billy, don't you ever put me in that situation again."

"Yes, ma'am." He was already on the stairs. The sound of his footsteps rose, moving farther away, and then Beth heard his bedroom door shut.

Beth had never lived in a two-story house before. Jim had never run an entire plant before. They had never belonged to a country club before, but the membership was both a perk and a duty of Jim's new job. Maybe one of these days they'd eat dinner there.

She expected Jim to call soon and ask how the fight had gone. Billy had been fretting about it for days, and even though Jim had given Billy boxing lessons, and sent him to karate classes, all to make up for his skinniness and clumsiness, when Jim learned that Billy was to fight Brian he told him to forget all that and just punch and keep punching. He had told Billy not to meet Brian any place he did not know; Jim had told Billy not to meet Brian any place he couldn't see his own house. Jim had seen boys agree to fight another boy, only to show up and find themselves fighting that boy and several of his friends, or fighting that boy and a baseball bat. Beth tried to tell Jim that such things didn't happen on cul-de-sacs, but he didn't want to take the chance.

Beth expected Jim would feel much like she did—disappointed that the fight had to happen, relieved that Billy had won, hopeful that Billy's misery in this town would stop now.

She knew that was what Billy wanted, not just not to be teased, but to be accepted, since as far as he knew violent skill had the final say when a man was judged. She had sometimes regretted the stories that Jim told, of being a rowdy boy, of being a football player, of being a Marine. She regretted them sometimes because they contradicted everything they expected their children to be: socialized, compassionate, earners of excellent grades. She regretted the stories sometimes because they all seemed to involve someone getting hurt, in one way or another. She understood, and appreciated, that a man was supposed to be tough: Jim was tough, her father was tough, Jim's father had been so tough that even other tough guys called him Tuffy. So she knew what Billy thought would happen now: an end to the picking, a start to kids liking him, since he'd now proved that he was tough, and the poor boy believed that tough was enough.

Beth had long ago noticed that Billy saw things that no one else did. She had also noticed that Billy, at twelve, didn't see the things everyone else did. She understood that Billy had had no choice, when Brian and his friends wouldn't stop picking on him, but to challenge him. She understood that the new kid in a town, a small town with very few new kids, a new kid who wore glasses and liked to read and was clumsy at sports, was going to be a target. She understood that Billy couldn't ignore it, couldn't keep walking away. That part she understood.

She did not understand why Jim made him fight where she would have to watch it. She did not understand why Jim had to protect his sons from dangers he imagined, or remembered, even as he told them to be tough and brave. She did not understand why Jim had worked so hard to move his family into a two-story house on a cul-de-sac in a subdivision, if he thought his sons would still face what he'd faced in the shadows of factories and mills. She did not understand what Jim thought it would do to her, watching her son hurt and be hurt by another boy, knowing she was not supposed to stop it.

Jim never called. He came home later than usual—ten or fifteen minutes only, not long enough to make her wonder, but long enough to make her notice. He walked into the kitchen through the same door through which Beth had watched the fight. Beth was cooking dinner, and the look on his face made her stop dicing a tomato.

"Hey," she said.

"Hey." He was still standing just inside the door, still holding his briefcase. He was not looking at her; he was watching her.

"He's all right," she said.

"What?"

What was wrong? "He's all right. Billy. He won the fight."

"He did?"

"I was afraid he was going to hurt the other boy. He had him down on the ground and kept on hitting him. I went out and stopped it."

"You stopped the fight?"

"I wasn't sure Billy was going to stop hitting that boy."

Jim stopped watching her. He looked out the window and curled his mouth the way he did when he had something to say he wasn't sure he should say.

"What's wrong?"

Jim shook his head. When he shook his head like that, Beth knew, he wasn't saying no, nothing's wrong; he wasn't saying that something was wrong but he would not burden her with his problems. When Jim shook his head like that, he was saying that something was going on, something big, but that he could handle it, and he would tell Beth about it so she could appreciate how much he was handling.

"Mac called this afternoon," Jim said. He set down his briefcase and sat down at the table. Beth turned the burner from medium to simmer. Mac was the president of Jim's company. She sat down next to her husband and he told her about Mac's call.

This is so stupid. This isn't just stupid; this is boring, and banal. This isn't even a real fight by any reasonable standard, just a silly schoolboy tussle fought for silly reasons at a silly location. If Billy becomes the kind of man his father is and his grandfathers were, he'll fight much more desperate battles than this, against grown men with full muscles and desperate intent. He'll have wars to fight, even, and if he remembers this at all he'll shake his head when he does, wondering why he wasted so much worry over something so silly and stupid and small. In a few months he might even live in another new town, where no one will have ever heard of Brian or this fight. If Jim gets the promotion Mac said he was up for, and moves us again, Billy can leave this town and all these boys behind, and never hear their names again. Maybe we can convince him that this won't happen in a new town, and he'll put all this in the deep, neglected place it deserves.

But this means all the world to him now, Beth reminded herself, and I'm his mother now as much as I will be then. Now is when he thinks he has to prove himself to everybody who judges him—his father, my father, his grandfather in heaven, the boys and girls at his school, himself. Everybody, Beth hoped, but me.

She reminded herself of this as she walked up the steps to his room, the day after the fight. He had burst through the door after school and run straight to his room, not stopping to say hi or grab something to eat, pushing Luke out of his way. Beth had heard his footsteps up the stairs, his bookbag slam to the floor, his body thrown onto his bed. She took a deep breath, followed, and knocked on his door.

Billy was trying hard not to cry. Finally he told her that everybody at school thought that he had lost the fight, because his mother had stopped it.

"Oh, Billy," she said, and then realized that she didn't know what else she could say.

The Wrecks of the Reconstruction

Holding Harvey's weight wasn't the issue; Jim Adams knew he could do that for as long as he needed to, even though Harvey was a big man. The issue was embarrassment. Not Harvey's, under the circumstances, and not Jim's at this display, but the embarrassment of all the men, co-workers and colleagues, standing nearby whom Harvey had not trusted with his weight. This, and not Harvey's tears, embarrassed Jim. Those other men walked in, and Harvey shook their hands, accepted their solid pats on his shoulders, kept his chin up. Jim walked in and Harvey threw his arms around him, would have collapsed, in tears, if Jim hadn't held him up, and Harvey had to have known that Jim would hold him up. Jim didn't even know Harvey all that well. So even though he could stand there all day holding Harvey up, he did not know how long he could stand there holding Harvey while all their colleagues—who had been at the visitation longer, saw Harvey more often, and knew him better—just stood by and saw.

Harvey's moment of collapse soon ended, though, and he straightened his back, grasping Jim by the shoulders before he took the handkerchief his tearful wife had been trying to hand him. With her left hand Linda rubbed Harvey's back while her right hand gripped, as best as it could, his sprawling upper arm.

"Thank you so much for being here, Jim," Harvey said.

"Don't you dare thank me, Harvey. It is the very least that I could do."

"It means a great deal to us," Linda said.

"I just wish I could do more. Beth is real sorry she can't be here."

"We understand," Linda said. "It's such a long drive."

"Naw, it's not that far." Jim put his hand on Linda's shoulder, as if to push himself away. Linda understood, put her hand over his, squeezed, and nodded. Jim turned to Harvey and struck him solidly, with an open hand, on the shoulder. Jim lowered his face a little as he raised his eyes to Harvey's—a coach's way of peering, of checking a rattled player to see if he could go back in the game. Harvey, old lineman that he was, knew the look and knew the short nod he was supposed to give. Jim again clapped him on the shoulder and moved away.

Jim had to go speak to Mac first, of course, ignoring all others along the way. Those he ignored weren't offended, unless they were young and ignorant. They cleared a path for him.

"Mac, how are you?"

"Oh, Jim, I honestly don't know," Mac said. "Something like this is hard to get your mind around."

"Yes it is."

"Not supposed to happen."

"No."

Now Jim could give attention and a firm handshake to the others, the other executive v-ps—north, east and west—and their plant managers, the comptrollers and counsels from the corporate office, the junior executives and sales managers he'd only met once or twice. Some of them were so eager, so lacking in soldierly, raise-the-drawbridge reserve, that Jim wanted to smack them.

"Mr. Adams, so good to see you again, sir."

"How was the drive up from Greenville, sir?"

"So how is South Carolina treating you, Mr. Adams?"

The other higher-ups tended to answer these kinds of questions loudly and crudely. Jim tended to answer with barely more than grunts, even when he wasn't in a funeral home and morally offended by their efforts to network. Conversations began around him, though, and grew comfortable. Jim was always amazed at how relaxed and familiar visitations became, and wasn't sure if that comforted him or disgusted him. A teenager woke up one morning feeling a little poorly, went to the doctor and took some tests; he came home with cancer and eight excruciating months to live. Like his father, Scott had been big and athletic, robust and capable. Mac was right, Mac was usually right—this was not supposed to happen.

Disconnected mourners came and went, more scared than mournful, more grateful than scared. They shook hands. They hugged. They broke apart into groups of people they already knew and talked, until they felt they'd been there long enough to go on. Scott's friends and teammates huddled in a side parlor, opposite the parlor where Harvey's co-workers gathered. Jim watched them when he could. They were sitting if they could. They kept their eyes on the floor. They were shaken and they weren't talking.

When he was ready to leave, Mac grabbed Jim by the elbow, interrupting a thirty-year-old sales manager who was reciting last month's figures.

"You're not heading straight back," Mac said, and maybe, Jim thought, Mac raised his voice enough at the end to make the sentence sound like a question.

"No," Jim said.

"Good. Why don't you come with me and let's get a drink."

They made their way to the sofa where Harvey and Linda were sitting now. The couple rose when Mac and Jim approached; Harvey shook their hands fiercely before they left.

They walked out into bright sunshine, the late afternoon, the crackle of Charlotte. Jim hated Charlotte, hated it more the more it grew. He had hated coming here twenty years ago to court Beth, and when her parents retired and moved back to Lincoln County, on the far side of Lake Norman from Charlotte, he was almost as glad as they were. He hated visiting the Charlotte office that Harvey ran; he hated that to get from Greenville to his mother's in Winston-Salem, you had to pass through Charlotte. Charlotte shuddered with aggression as it spread; soon it would be as big as Atlanta, and Jim found its air hard to breathe.

Mac pointed along Providence Road. "There's a bar down here on the left. You can follow me."

The bar was full of expensive suits in various stages—jackets slung over chairs or held with a hooked finger over a shoulder, ties loosened, collar buttons undone. Gold glittered—watches, class and wedding rings, cufflinks. A few youngish men wore bright suspenders. Mac and Jim were expensively suited, but they wore their suits in the way that suited Mac—as if they had earned their gray suits not through connections and degrees, but through years of hard work, cunning, and command.

They took a table in the corner and Mac ordered Jack Daniels on the rocks for both of them. Mac insisted that any male in his employ above the level of counter salesman drink only straight liquor if they were drinking with him; wine was allowed for fancy dinners, and beer was accepted on the golf course. He insisted that anyone in management play golf, and they'd be better off if they played it well. He insisted that the men in sales and in the corporate office have earned, at the very least, a high school varsity letter in a sport that required throwing a ball. Exceptional cunning with numbers, though, could make him relax this unwritten rule.

Mac shook his head as they waited for their drinks to arrive. "Sad thing. Awful. Burying a child. Supposed to be the other way around."

"I hate to even think about it," Jim said. Mac looked at him, irritated, and leaned forward. He was getting hard of hearing, despite how hard he hated it, and Jim's voice fell to a rumbling growl when he was thoughtful or sad. Jim repeated himself, louder.

"Let's don't think about it then," Mac almost shouted. "How's your family?"

"Fine. Fine. Beth's keeping herself busy. Billy just sent in his application to Wake, so he's already checking the mailbox three times a day." Jim paused to thank the waitress who brought their drinks.

"He still playing basketball?"

"That's Luke. He's the ballplayer. Billy ran track for a while, but he got a job at the local newspaper and didn't have time for both. Maggie just finished first grade and wants a horse."

"Don't they all?" Mac said, and laughed. "They all like Greenville, huh?"

Four years after you sent me there is a little late to ask, Jim thought. "Yeah, we love it. Real nice people. Not too big."

"Not like Charlotte."

"No, not at all like Charlotte. It's funny, growing up in North Carolina you always hate to like anything about South Carolina, but Greenville's awfully nice."

"Good, good." Mac took a long sip of his drink, longer than usual. Jim noticed, looked away from him, and waited.

"I wanted to tell you in person, Jim," Mac said, "the family's got a real good offer on the table."

"How good?" Jim was still looking away.

Mac shrugged. "Maybe not as good as it could be, but goddamn hard to walk away from."

"You think they could get more?"

"No, it's not that. The money's not the hard part."

"All the rest of it, then?"

"Yeah. All the rest. The future."

Jim nodded, and, at last, faced Mac.

"Who's the offer from?"

"The New Yorkers."

Mac used "the New Yorkers" as a code, because there was more than one interested party based in Manhattan. But "the New Yorkers" was used only for the Wall Street arbitrage firm that had almost bought the company on the last go-round, the one that made no secret of its intentions. Everybody in management knew what the New Yorkers would do with controlling interest. The family, the ancient widow and three elderly children of the founder, knew what the New Yorkers would do, too, but everybody in management also knew that the family was eager to get shy of the business. At board meetings the widow and her children looked over their shoulders, and spoke ominously of Japanese invasion.

"The family gets to do what they think is best," Jim said.

"Yes, they do."

"Have they asked you what you think is best?"

"Well, yeah," Mac said. Mac had been hired by the founder when one plant was open, in Greensboro. He had been CEO since the founder died, had orchestrated two decades of bold expansion—across the Carolinas, and then out across the Southeast, and then out into the Sun Belt and the Midwest. Mac had insisted, as they grew, on keeping Carolina in the company name, to remind their own people and give them pride in where they came from, to remind the Texas and Ohio and Pennsylvania big shots as to who was eating their lunch.

"We've talked on several occasions," Mac said. He leaned back in his seat, away from Jim; he raised his left hand a little off the table, pulling his fingers back, stretching them as far as he could, making a defensive, almost a conciliatory gesture, and in that gesture Jim could see the future and the past.

Mac's holdings in the company were almost as big as the family's. He wouldn't sell to the New Yorkers directly, Jim knew, but he would cash in when the price shot up, and Mac couldn't help it if the New Yorkers were waiting at the other end of the investment banks, could he?

"I told them they had to look at the kind of money now on the table," Mac was saying. Jim could almost hear himself speaking on the factory floor of any or every one of the plants in his region. The New Yorkers would start on the periphery, which for Jim would mean trips to Birmingham, Jacksonville, Chattanooga. They'd let go of the truck drivers first and contract out the shipping. Then warehouse labor, secretaries, counter sales, custodians would hear from Jim's own mouth that their long service was appreciated but no longer needed. Then the survivors would gather outside the plant while Jim stood on the loading dock and told them they had six—weeks? months?—more until the plant closed and they fell through the flimsy floor of the working class.

"They need to look at what's in their best long-term interest," Mac said, and Jim wouldn't have argued. The company would be streamlined, not for efficiency and certainly not for growth, but for resale. With enough expense off the books the stock price would almost have to rise. Their purpose, the end at which they aimed, would no longer be to build or to make, but to be sold. Jim wondered if everything that truly needed to be made, in this country, had been. He had long thought about building his own company, the way his grandfather did. His grandfather had left the farm with a sixth grade education and a country boy's knack for tools, and made himself a contractor.

"Simple economic realities," Mac was saying, and Jim didn't disagree. When it came time to build, you built; when it came time to sell, you sold. Granddaddy saw he could make a better living laying brick and concrete block, so he laid brick and concrete block. When he saw that more bricks were being laid down in Winston, he moved his family down to Winston.

"Just the way the world is right now," Mac was saying. "Look right here around us, at what's going on in Charlotte. These banks are going like gangbusters, because they can supply what the current market needs more than anything—cash."

I've looked around Charlotte all I want to, Jim thought.

Beth's father got out of the service and found a job he knew nothing about, just like Jim had. Beth's father sold truck parts—counter sales—until he caught a lucky break. His boss offered him his own franchise if he'd move down to Charlotte and put up $2000. Then he caught another lucky break, when his father-in-law fronted him the $2000. Then he caught his third and biggest break, when the government built not one but two interstate highways through Charlotte. They crossed just north of the center of the city, and John Gardiner had his shop in the crotch. While Jim's father was still laying brick, Beth's father was figuring out that moving things across town, across the state, across the country was the way to grow. Moving parts wear out fast.

Jim had caught a few breaks himself. A cousin had brought him into the Winston-Salem plant to get a job as a draftsman, drawing bridges and steel structures on graph paper for the rest of his life. Still in his Marine Corps buzzcut, Jim answered all the plant manager's questions easily, until he was asked "You're Will Adams's boy, aren't you?"

"Yes, sir, I am."

"I played football with him at Hanes. Best ballplayer I ever saw, pound for pound. You play football?"

"Yes, sir, I did."

"You as good as your daddy?"

"No, sir."

"How'd you like a job on the sales counter?" In ten years Jim was the sales manager. In twenty he was a vice president.

"Natural progression," Mac was saying.

But sometimes, Jim thought, the natural progression falls apart. His grandfather had wanted Jim to carry on the contracting business, but Jim wanted other things. Harvey's only child died; John Gardiner tried to manufacture heirs to carry on his company, but none of them could do the job.

"I need to head back to Greensboro soon," Mac was saying, "before I-85 becomes a parking lot."

Two interstates crossed in Charlotte, a city where you had to be in motion and in a hurry. Jim had resisted it, had tried to stay in the red brick steadfastness of Winston-Salem. Instead he had been transferred twice, both times a promotion, each time further from home. He had circled Charlotte. John Gardiner had never really liked him much, but John knew what Jim could do.

"You're right, Mac," Jim said. "There's nothing but road work from here to the state line. I best get a move on."

War Orphan

He ran down the steps from the bus and leapt to the curb, as a child will when he gives up to gravity. Joe Simms would remember admiring the kid's guts then. The boy was only five years old.

Joe's wife Stacia stepped forward to meet him while Joe stayed back with their daughter. Stacia went to one knee, to the boy's level. She shook his little hand with a smile, and squeezed his little shoulder with warmth. The boy, Joe saw, had a long, aggressive smile, and Joe saw that his wife was captivated.

An attendant behind the boy asked Stacia for a photo ID, for which Stacia rummaged in her purse. Their daughter, Sally, went from rising on her toes to hopping from foot to foot. Joe laid a gentle hand on the back of Sally's neck and shoulders; she had just turned four, and Joe knew she couldn't be expected to stand still for this long. Sally stopped hopping, but trembled and shook beneath Joe's hand.

Her identity proven, Stacia took the boy's bag from off his back and replaced it with her hand, guiding him to Joe and Sally. The boy moved slowly. His smile wasn't half as long.

To Joe he used "sir" and "please." To Sally he used a wondrous, confident "hey" and an easy laugh. Joe looked at his wife, and fears seemed to slide off her face. Joe held the boy's hand to the car.

The boy was the son of Stacia's sister Macy, and his name was Jordan. Jordan was born a couple of years after Macy had run off to Atlanta. Stacia's family didn't know much about Jordan's father, and they didn't know that they knew everything Macy did. He dealt coke. He dealt a lot of it, to judge by the clothes and cars he had heaped on Macy, and by the 25 years the Feds had smacked him with. So what if he dealt coke, Macy had cried, he was good to her and had said he would take care of her and the baby. He just dealt coke, she had cried, because he came up real hard. He just dealt coke, she had cried, because he wasn't going to work no shit job and he wasn't going to take no shit from no man. He had needed to provide for his family when he was just 13, and what else was he going to do at 13? They won't even let you work at Burger King when you're only 13.

Joe would have none of that, but he kept quiet when Stacia's family gathered to discuss Macy. He had spent all of his 13th summer in his grandfather's tobacco field. Joe, just like his grandfather, never had much use for excuses.

Macy's family built an image of her life with Jordan. They gathered materials from different sources, from Stacia and her brother and her father. Each piece arrived on-site, sitting at the ready until put to use. Macy somehow kept a nice apartment in Midtown. The Feds had impounded the car Jordan's father had bought her, but she soon had another that was more than serviceable. She mentioned new boyfriends. She sometimes asked her father for money, but not as often as he thought a waitress with a Midtown apartment should. She confessed to her brother that she had once left her bedroom to find Jordan on top of the refrigerator; she let slip to Stacia that she had once left her bedroom to find Jordan in the kitchen with the butcher knife.

Her family measured each piece against probability, their own experience in the world, and Macy's history of half-truths. They assembled a strong structure, and then decided they should take Jordan from Macy and send him to live with Stacia and Joe. Stacia redesigned the guest room into a boy's bedroom, registered Jordan for kindergarten at Rock Springs Elementary School and bought him a backpack. Joe and his father-in-law each offered to drive to

Atlanta, but Macy told them both they didn't have to. She would not give her address. She told Stacia she would get Jordan to her. She called back later with his bus number and arrival time.

The drive from the bus station in Charlotte back to Rock Springs was not long, but took them west across the Catawba. As he drove Joe told Jordan the story, how his ancestors had come to North Carolina as indentured servants long before the Revolution. Just as soon as they'd done their time, Joe said, they came up here to Lincoln County to settle their own land. Joe's people had been here ever since. He made it sound easy and inevitable.

"I came here from Atlanta," Jordan said.

"Yep," Joe said.

"I came here in a bus."

"We know, boy, we were there."

"Oh. Am I going to be here forever?"

Joe and Stacia laughed, but not for long. "Well, honey," Stacia said, "you'll be here until you're grown. Then you can go wherever you want to."

"Oh. I'll go when I'm grown. Cool, is that a GameBoy?"

Sally didn't look up. "Yeah. It's mine."

"Cool. Can I play it sometime?"

"Sure."

"Can I play it now?"

"No, I'm playing it now."

"Can I play it when you're done?"

"I guess."

"When will you be done?"

"I don't know."

"Okay, but I can play with it when you're done?"

"Yes."

"Okay." He smiled at Sally, his smile long and aggressive again.

Joe Simms was a builder. He was a sub-contractor. He was a mason.

The next morning he was awake and out of the house before

dawn. On Highway 16 and Slanting Bridge Road he drove northeast to Lake Norman. He crossed the lake as the sun rose. A mist came up off the water and rolled onto the bridge. At Sherrills Ford he turned right, and drove to the end of a small peninsula. In a lot facing the leeward cove, a timbered frame rose three stories. Hector and his crew were waiting.

He was glad to see that the bricks and mortar he had ordered were waiting. He pulled his truck up onto the lot and set the crew to work. Joe was methodical and absolute on how things should be done, but Hector had worked with him several times since the previous spring. He was familiar with Joe's method, with what should go where. Joe gave orders in English, which Hector translated into Spanish.

Two men began to unload the scaffolding from the bed of Joe's truck. They stacked the pipes where Joe, through Hector, directed, with a stack at each corner of the house. Two men snapped the bindings off the skidloads of bricks, removing them and restacking them in wheelbarrows, and carting them to piles built on each of the house's four sides. Two men broke into the mortar, fetched water from the tank in the bed of Joe's truck, and began mixing.

Once this work was begun, Joe let Hector supervise the crew while he inspected the timber, the sheet rock, and the foundation he'd laid a couple of weeks before. The timber frame seemed straight and sturdy, and the sheet rock seemed well hung. The foundation appeared uncracked and even. Joe smiled at the prospect of a good job.

Joe returned home to unusual noise: Sally and Jordan screaming in the back yard. Joe walked around the side of his house.

Sally was chasing Jordan; or, rather, Jordan was letting Sally chase him. Sally was not very much smaller. Jordan was faster, but less in control of his body. He stumbled and fell often, though Joe noticed that he knew how to fall and did not cry.

Standing still by the corner, Joe was able to watch for a while before they saw him. When they did Jordan ran to him.

"Sally's trying to get me," he said. He was laughing.

"Don't let that girl scare you," Joe said, smiling. He patted Jordan's shoulder and pushed him lightly back toward Sally.

"He wanted me to chase him," Sally said from across the yard. Jordan ran over to her. He stopped directly in front of her, his arm's length away, but then slid sideways and closer, facing her at 45 degrees. He had given her room to move, to advance, but not to avoid him entirely. She walked forward, watching him from the corner of her eye, her arm brought up against her chest. Jordan moved with her every step.

Joe, watching him, thought he remembered something, some game.

"Y'all play nice now," he said, and walked inside.

Watching the news that night, Joe remembered chess. His father had taught him, but he hadn't played since he was a teenager. He remembered the way a pawn took another piece—sidling, and at an angle.

"I think Sally enjoys having him here," Stacia said. "It's nice for her to have someone to play with."

Joe stacked the dishes by the sink.

"It might be hard sometimes, getting used to not being the only child. But that's just part of growing up," Stacia said.

Joe finished stacking, grunted, and ran the hot water.

"I know it's been hard for me sometimes," Stacia said. "Two's a lot harder than one."

"I bet," Joe said.

"I'm sure it's going to be all right, though," Stacia said.

Joe smiled at her. She came closer, and he kissed her, leaving his soapy hands in the sink. "I love you," he said.

Joe kept his weekends filled. Clear Saturdays he was fishing at dawn, sitting on his cooler by the river. He always quit by mid-morning, though, leaving himself time for yardwork and repairs. If he finished those in time he'd let himself watch football, basketball, or baseball, depending on the season. Stacia kept his dinner warm for him if the game was good and ran long. Every Sunday morning they went to church, and then went out for a big lunch. Joe had pleasant pictures in his mind of bringing Jordan into this routine.

That Saturday morning Joe disabled the airbag in his truck so Jordan could sit in the front seat next to him. The child curled around his seatbelt, sleeping. He woke up slowly at the river.

Sally approached her mother in the kitchen.

"Jordan was using some bad words to me yesterday," she said.

Stacia looked down at her daughter. "Like what?"

"Real bad ones. I don't want to say."

"Good. Don't," Stacia said. "If your father or I hears Jordan using bad words, we'll deal with it. But, honey, do you know what a tattletale is?"

Sally stared.

"Nobody likes a tattletale. A tattletale is someone who tells on somebody else when they don't have to. So you just let us worry about Jordan and don't be telling on him. Okay, sweetie?"

The lure broke the film of the water, creating ripples that collapsed in on the center, rather than moving out. The hook glistened in the sun as it flew toward shore. Joe ducked. The lure sailed over his head. The hook stuck with a thump in a tree.

"What are you doing?" Joe asked Jordan.

Jordan laughed.

"That ain't funny."

Jordan stopped laughing, and held his lips tightly together.

Joe stared at the boy, controlling his temper. He realized how soft the boy's face was. Jordan smiled at him, smiled for him, a long and aggressive come-on. Joe would later swear the boy batted his eyes. Joe found himself thinking of Macy's face and Macy's body until he shook such thoughts away.

"You do it right, like I showed you, or we'll go on back now," Joe said.

Macy called. She talked for a long time to Stacia about Jordan, before asking to speak to him. They talked for only a few minutes. Macy talked to Stacia some more, while Stacia's face drew tight and her voice grew strained.

Stacia's father called often, and sent checks and presents for Jordan through the mail. Jordan sat smiling, in wonder at all his riches.

Months passed. Macy didn't call again.

"You did, you did mean to. You did."

"No I didn't. No I didn't." Jordan looked frantically at Sally's bedroom door.

"Yes, you did. You did, too. I told you not to but you did."

"But I didn't hear you."

Stacia came in from the kitchen to investigate.

"What happened?"

"He just, he, he …"

"Okay, honey, okay. Jordan, you want to tell me what happened?"

"Nothing."

"Nothing? This is nothing?"

Jordan was silent. He played with his fingers and looked sideways at the floor.

"It's obvious something happened, Jordan, so why don't you tell me what?"

That night, in bed, when Stacia, exasperated, told Joe about it, she would swear to him that, then, while she waited with growing anger for him to answer her, Jordan, it seemed, was trying hard, she swore, not to smile.

In late September Stacia met with Jordan's teachers.

"His teachers said Jordan's doing very well at school," Stacia told Joe at dinner that night. Jordan smiled at Joe.

"They said he's very bright, and learns very quickly," Stacia said.

"That doesn't surprise me at all," Joe said.

"They said he does need to work on his listening," Stacia said, "and on not talking during class."

"Yeah," Jordan said, "I'm going to work on those things."

The four of them arrived at Stacia's father's house on Christmas Eve. The children ran up the driveway to him. Stacia's father swept Jordan up in his arms.

"Merry Christmas, sport."

"Merry Christmas, Poppy," Jordan screamed.

"Is Santa going to be good to you this year?"

"Uh-huh."

"Have you been a good boy this year?"

"Uh-huh. I have been."

"Good."

He lowered Jordan, who watched as he picked up Sally.

Inside Jordan jumped into a ring of wrapped gifts. He spun, laughing and shrieking, and then Sally did the same. Joe and Stacia, once each, told them to stop, but no one listened. Stacia's father watched over the children and laughed along with them.

Later the children were in bed. Stacia's father and stepmother were in large recliners. Stacia and Joe were on the couch. Joe sipped the bourbon and water he had learned, over the years, to accept.

"It's so sad," Stacia's stepmother said. "Macy was always such a sweet little thing. From the time I knew her."

"I know it's got to be hard for y'all sometimes," Stacia's father said to her.

"It's hard all the time," Stacia said. She pushed her hair from her face. "Raising Sally's hard. But it's just with Jordan, he's so . . . I mean, all the time . . ."

"Well," Stacia's father said, "Jordan's a different child than Sally."

Damn right, Joe thought.

"I know that, Dad," Stacia said. "But he's just—we can't trust him. He's always making stuff up, telling us stories, making excuses. He didn't go on a field trip 'cause he forgot to bring the note home, then told his teachers that we wouldn't sign it. His teachers think we're awful. I have to stay on him all the time, for everything."

"Well, kids do things like that. All kids tell stories."

"No, it's more than that." Stacia looked at the Christmas tree.

The words, for everything the boy drained from them, were unavailable to her. "I mean, the child just does not listen. You tell him not to do something, and he gets this stupid little grin on his face. He really doesn't care about anybody else or anybody else's feelings. The way he picks on Sally …"

"Oh, you're one to talk," Stacia's stepmother said laughing. "I remember how you used to pick on your brother and sister. You were horrible to them."

"I know I was," Stacia said, "but Jordan is different."

"I remember one time we were talking about how sweet Macy was, and you said, 'She's just pretending to be sweet, one of these days you're going to find out how evil she really is.' How awful! What an awful thing to say about your sister, Stacia! And y'all were just kids. Macy was such a little doll back then." She laughed.

"Stacia and Macy were always very different people," their father said.

"Thank God," Joe said. He checked his bourbon.

Later still Joe tried to sleep. He kept remembering the one picture he'd seen of Macy and Jordan together. They were both leaning into the camera, making demands of the composition. They had the same smile.

All that evening he'd remembered incidents they could have told Stacia's parents about. He'd remembered the afternoon Jordan broke Sally's dollhouse, the one Joe had built himself, and he'd remembered how Jordan did not seem to care once he realized that no one would hit him. He'd remembered Jordan walking into the bathroom while Stacia showered because he wanted something to drink, happy to sit there until she came out. He'd remembered many of the times that Jordan had scared or grabbed or touched or just kept on talking to Sally, driving her one way or another to scream. Jordan once slipped behind the counter at the grocery store, while the cashier was bagging and Stacia was writing a check, and began playing with the register. Stacia screamed at him to stop, and he laughed; the cashier told him to stop, and he laughed. Stacia reached over the counter, picked up Jordan and popped him on the leg. Jordan laughed.

They could give this child all the love and attention they possessed, and he'd just eat it up and smile. He'd burp and be hungry for more. If Joe could've said it, he might've done something about it. With each day he felt more sure that Macy and her child were stealing something from them. He'd love the child ferociously, but it would do no good.

He kept thinking of his father, who had died two days after his heart attack, while Joe was away in the Army and could do little more than come back for the funeral. He kept thinking of his mother, stuck mindless in a nursing home near Newton. He kept thinking of how much more Sally used to smile. He tried again to sleep. He kept hearing Stacia trying not to cry.

A cold wind came off the lake, clean and painful. Joe stood at the windward edge of a shallow cove. He had finished a house here, a two-story Colonial. He stood on the shore and looked across the water at the last house he'd built, which was sitting empty until early summer. To the south, facing another cove, was the house he'd begun that morning. He'd spent the day breaking in a new crew, local boys, half-assed and silly. He heard a car door slam.

I wish right now, Joe thought, that I was in a shallow draft boat, alone with a veteran dog, hunting ducks.

"Beautiful," the contractor said. "Just beautiful, Joe."

"Thank you."

"I mean it, Joe. You do great work for me."

"I do my best."

"Everything go all right?"

"Fine. I had a good crew."

"And you came in right at budget." The contractor shook his head. "Outstanding. Joe, I couldn't be happier. Far as I'm concerned, you are my guy."

"I appreciate that."

"No, I mean it, Joe."

They both stared at the Colonial. The contractor zipped up his windbreaker. Joe looked at the country club crest over the contractor's heart.

"So you like that crew you use?" the contractor asked.

"I do. They're excellent."

"Really? What's his name, the guy …"

"Hector Melendez."

"He easy to manage?"

"He doesn't need to be managed. He knows what he's doing."

"Really?"

Joe nodded.

"Think they might be interested in more than brick work?"

"Might. But they're gone now."

"Really?"

Joe nodded again. "Moved on. More work other places. I think they headed down to the coast."

"Really?"

Joe turned back to the water.

"That house is a beaut," the contractor said. "The owners are going to be thrilled."

"They should get a lot of good years out of it," Joe said.

The contractor smiled. He reached into his jacket.

"Well, I can't say you haven't earned it."

Joe thanked him for the check.

When Joe got home Stacia was in the kitchen, cooking dinner and ignoring the noise in the basement. Joe walked up behind her and kissed her on the cheek.

"Hey," she said.

"Hey. How was your day?"

"Fine."

"What are the kids doing?"

"I don't know," she said tightly. She sliced an onion. "They're downstairs."

Joe took off his jacket and hung it on the back of a chair.

"I'll go see."

Joe walked downstairs.

Halfway down the steps he could hear Jordan talking, loudly, almost yelling. At the bottom of the steps he could hear Sally crying.

Sally was in the corner and Jordan was in front of her, facing her, looking down at her as she cowered and cried. He spoke loudly as she cried. "Why won't you, Sally? Why won't you do that?" He asked again and pulled her towards him until he saw her see her father. Jordan spun around, let go of Sally, and put his back against the wall next to her. Sally stood still as her father closed in on Jordan.

"What are you doing?" Joe shouted. He grabbed Jordan by the arm and jerked him to the middle of the room.

Jordan looked down and away. His lips came together, full, their corners curled up. Joe was aware of a half-formed thought before he struck Jordan with his hand.

The boy fell sideways to his knees. His eyes were open and stunned. He put both hands on his cheek. He made no sound.

Joe had thoughts of shaking him, throwing him against a wall, and of the enormous satisfaction he'd get watching that decadent little body crumble to the floor. He glared down at the boy, whose eyes narrowed, and who began to cry in soft pulses. The pulses became tight sobs, and Joe listened to their desperate edge.

Joe heard Sally crying. She was still in the corner. She cried in long, fearful whines. Joe heard Stacia enter the room. He turned to her, and held up his hand before she could speak.

The Survivors

To let anyone pass, Kate Sawyer had to pull her delicate legs up to her chest. She pulled her legs up slowly, and though she was keeping them from the party, no one who waited seemed to mind. The grace with which Kate moved was often and lustily praised, but Will Adams knew that she was just careful to move slowly, in a closely guarded way, and that these days that was, though heartbreaking, enough. She and Will sat next to each other in a concrete stairwell in a corner of a dorm, their backs against the wall, smoking cigarettes and drinking beer. Sean McManus sat across from them, against the railing, holding his guitar. They were just far enough from the party to hear each other. They talked about their summer jobs.

"These kids we had," Sean said, "you just couldn't believe what their homes were like."

"I know," Kate said. "I'm convinced that the week they spent at our camp was the first week some of these kids had gone in their entire lives without getting beaten."

"Oh," Sean said, "no doubt."

"I mean, they were good kids, most of them, but coming from a home life like that, where you feel like everybody's out to get you . . ."

"Of course you do," said Sean, "everybody *is* out to get you."

"You don't trust anybody," Kate said.

"You've got to stand up for yourself constantly," Sean said. "Constantly."

"We spent the first, like, three days of each week just trying to convince the kids that nobody here was going to hurt them. No matter what they did."

"And some you never can convince," Sean said. "It's frustrating as shit."

More and more students, in lighthearted tee shirts and khaki shorts, climbed the steps between them. The three of them talked on about their summers, unbothered. Will tried to listen and compose at the same time, calling up the memories of all his vivid senses and trying to fit them into something of interest. He had not been a camp counselor; he had not reached out to troubled kids. He had delivered truck parts for his dad. He and some other friends had almost signed up to work on a fishing boat in Alaska, but his dad had talked him out of that. Instead he drove all summer, up and down industrial streets, through all the dirty trade routes of north and west Charlotte. He kicked up dust in truckyards, and in the sunlight watched it settle slowly down, surrounded by turbines and pistons, big machines making or moving things. He got used to the smell of burnt oil. He loaded his truck with brake shoes in interlocking stacks, and by the end of the summer he could carry a stack of four shoes in each arm. He still had calluses on his hands and grease underneath his nails. The party above them grew and grew louder, and Will expected that they'd go back to it soon. He expected that Kate would go back in soon. He had to put together something good, something persuasive, and he had to do it soon. Kate and Sean raised the stakes.

"I had this one boy, the second week I was there," Kate said, "aim his bow and arrow right at my chest from about one foot away, and we both just stood there, like …"

"Jesus," Sean said.

"But by the end of the week," she said, "he was crying on my shoulder, saying how he didn't want to go home."

"We had a twelve-year-old," Sean said, "steal a knife from the woodworking shop and pull it on another kid. I ran over and got between them; I used my best Dad-voice and said, 'Give me that,' and held my hand out. He looked at me for a minute like, 'Motherfucker, I'm gonna cut that hand off you don't get it out of my face.' I just kept standing there. I think he finally realized he didn't want to go back to juvie so he gave me the knife."

"Did you have any trouble with the locals around your camp?" Kate asked.

"A little," Sean said.

"I was leading my group of kids on a hike," Kate said, "and we got to this clearing where we were going to take a break. But there were about four or five guys there, that looked like they were around 16 or so, with beer cans all over the place. And I could smell pot in the air. They started talking shit to the campers, calling them really awful names, so I told the kids to turn around and go straight back to camp.

"I went last to make sure all the kids got away. One of these guys starts coming toward me going, 'Hey, you're sexy,' and all this shit so I just" - Kate raised her middle finger—"and said, 'Fuck you,' and took off."

Will's face turned red because Kate was looking at him. Kate was looking at him because she knew what things she had told him before. Over the summer she wrote him letters in response to his. They sorted out exactly what they felt for each other in the highest words they had available. She wrote that she loved him, but he knew what she meant. Will said he could live with that. Saying so made him feel noble. He read *The Return of the Native* again and saw himself as the reddleman Diggory Venn, biding strongly by for Tamsin while Wildeve failed her time after time until he died at the end of the book. Except that he knew Kate's boyfriend, and could not see him failing her, not in the ways that Will would.

"Our camp was on a river," Sean said, "way down in the eastern part of the state. I used to take a canoe out whenever I had a break and go explore the river and the swamps and these little creeks. One time I was on the riverbank when these guys came up and asked if I could squeal like a pig, but other than that . . ." They all laughed, and with a big grin Kate flipped off Sean. Sean told them, though, about the alligators he'd see briefly on the surface, and how they'd glide back down slowly, beneath the green scum on top of the water, until even the few ripples they made were gone. He talked about banks so crowded with gnarled trees that they seemed to swallow the river. He joked about his nagging worry, when he was in the river's deepest reaches and most secluded coves, that he was about to stumble onto some monster, something prehistoric, some freak of survival. "And you know what's really fucked up," he said, "is that I never did—and it never made me feel any better."

Will smiled and said he knew the feeling. He hastily reviewed and assembled. On top of an interstate bridge he'd driven by a family, a father, a mother, and three blonde children, who held signs that said they were out of work and food. When he saw their eyes he was afraid they would step into traffic or jump over the guardrails. He did not stop, though; he had to a job to do for his father. On the corner of Craighead and Graham Streets he'd seen the woman say something to the man in the pickup truck, negotiate, and get in. He'd seen women at their jobs with bruises no amount of makeup could cover. From these he had to make a parable: I have seen enough, Kate, to justify myself.

She must have thought so, once, or she wouldn't have trusted him like she did. She wouldn't have kissed him, once, quickly, on the lips, in the parking lot of a grocery store, as a thank you for the flower Will bought her on impulse. He almost staggered then. That a girl as exquisite as Kate could like him, like that, had never occurred to him. Some remarkable kindness about her, beyond her face, her voice, and her body, made guys fall all over her. In the summer Will listened to some of the guys talk back in the shop, and he realized then that she'd given him chances. He'd missed them all, being chivalrous, being a boy. Why he thought he might have a chance now he did not know, but he put some thoughts together and spoke. "Where I worked this summer, delivering truck parts, every now and then you'd hear random gunfire just off in the distance, you know, like just a few blocks away," Will said. "Everybody'd duck, and, like, a lot of the guys I worked with carried a gun. Some of 'em would have to hide if a police car passed by, 'cause they were actually wanted for shit. One guy didn't show up for work one Monday, so we called his house. His girlfriend said she'd called the cops on him Sunday night, 'cause he'd come back so drunk he'd gone into the crawlspace and started barking like a dog." Kate and Sean laughed, but Will could tell he'd missed what was crucial. They were unswayed as to the worthiness of his summer's work. He might have seen as much or more than they had, but all he had done was watch. His work might even have been dangerous, but Will knew that what they were all really looking for was not just a thrill but a righteous test—a great crusade, or a bad one to protest, not the ambiguous scraps left to them. The three of them had grown up comfortable, guarded from what they felt should be theirs. They had done or had seen some crazy shit—pranks that got way out of hand, bungee jumps, guys who hiked solo into deep, dark woods. Will knew a guy who had backpacked from Hong Kong to Helsinki. What the crazy shit boasted in risk or knowledge, though, it lacked in justice. Will recognized a hopeful, almost awestruck tone that Kate and Sean used to describe their summer jobs. He got the feeling they were each talking to themselves as much as to each other, and to their mothers and fathers even more.

"Are you going back next year?" Kate asked Sean.

"I don't know. I'd like to. I may need to look for an internship or something, you know?"

"Yeah. I want to go back, too, but I don't know if I'll be able to."

"Yeah."

The door above them swung open and the stairwell rattled with noise. Paul Sorriano walked out onto the landing. A pert blonde sophomore followed him, while a couple of guys and a couple of girls stuck their heads out the open door. "The fuck you guys doing down there?" Sorriano asked, but not really. "Party's in here." He took a handful of ice from his cup and threw it at them. He was looking at Kate.

Kate and Sean picked up the scattered, liquor-scented cubes and, grinning, threw them back. Will picked up a bottlecap by his side and snapped it at Sorriano's head.

"Get your asses in here," Sorriano called, throwing more ice. Sean jumped to his feet and charged up the stairs at him, holding his guitar by its neck like a weapon. Sorriano opened the door and much laughter was heard.

Kate stood up and wiped the dust from her ass. She turned to Will and smiled. "Come on," she said, and held out a dainty hand. She pretended to pull him to his feet.

Intercession

The three of them were standing behind the parts counter talking about the pile one of them had won on the golf course. Ken Murphy, the boss, saw her first, saw her and watched her closely, in fact, but as a habit he waited to tell anyone anything. Davey Dockett sometimes waited, but not this time, and he saw her next. Davey pointed her out by saying, "Will you look at this here."

She walked with a steady pace and an uneven gait up Statesville Road, walking away from Statesville Avenue, the city, and the I-85 interchange. She was small but she looked kind of thick, and her hair was cut as short as a man's. That she was not a man could be seen, through her jacket, her thickness and her distance. Ricky Jordan, who played golf but never for money, grimaced. Davey watched her as he shook his head.

Davey and Ricky went back to debating why Ricky never played for money, but Ken kept his eye on the girl.

"I can play," Ricky said. "It ain't that. I know I can play."

"That so?"

"Me and my daddy, and my brother, and his brother-in-law, we all went out Saturday and played. I was stroking it that day, too, boy. Hoo."

"So why don't you come on out with me sometime?" Davey asked.

Ken realized she was heading for his shop.

"Nah," Ricky said. "That's too far for me to drive on a Saturday."

"Shit, Tom Waddell drove down from Lincolnton."

"He did?"

"He did," Davey said. "He wishes he didn't, but he did."

"You tee him up?"

"Teed him up. Three rounds and he was done."

"Took him for all he had?" Ricky asked.

"You see this big ol' bulge in my back pocket, don't you?" Davey asked as he slapped his wallet on the counter. "Matches the big ol' bulge in my front pocket."

She left the side of Statesville Road and started to cross Starita Road, and Ken could see that her face was discolored and swollen. When she had crossed Starita Road and set foot on the gravel outside the delivery door, he could see that someone had beaten the hell out of her.

She walked up the ramp and Ken straightened and faced the counter. Davey and Ricky looked around, saw her, and disappeared into the back office.

"Mister, can you help me?" she asked as she came through the door.

"What's the problem?" Ken asked her. Her hands and her head were shaking and she was breathing hard. She was half his size but he felt unsafe.

"You gotta help me. I need help. Please, you gotta help me."

"Now, wait a minute …"

"You –"

"Wait a –"

"You got to –"

"a minute, what –"

"help me –"

"What's the –"

"help me please –"

"problem, what's –"

"please mister –"

"Wait –"

"My girlfriend and me, we was staying at the motel down the

road and we had a fight this morning and she hit me with the telephone and knocked me out cold and she left me and took the car and all our money and we was going to New York together and she took the money and I don't know what I'm gonna do I'm from Atlanta and my parents my parents kicked me out and I came up here and …"

Ken let her talk because it gave him time to think. What would she want him to do for her? He assumed she was lying; everyone who walked in off Statesville Road was lying. She was wearing a thick Army jacket when it was eighty degrees outside. She could have a gun. He had a rifle. He had a rifle, back in his office.

"So what do you want from me?"

"Mister, I just need thirty dollars, thirty dollars is all I need so I can get me a room to stay in till my parents come and get me tomorrow. Please, mister, you got to help me out, I just need thirty dollars …"

"Wait a minute …"

"Please, mister –"

"Wait." The girl stopped when Ken spoke like that. "I'm not going to just give you thirty dollars."

"What do you mean? I just need it to get a room for one night, please, I've been walking up and down this road and ain't nobody given me nothing and all I need's a room for one night till my daddy comes to get me. Please, mister, don't make me …"

"Wait just a minute. Calm down."

"But mister –"

"Calm down." She did. "Wait right here, you understand? Wait right here."

Ken went into the back office and sent Ricky out to keep an eye on her. Ricky watched her from behind a tall stack of boxes whose labels he pretended to read.

The secretary, Nancy, was standing with Davey just inside the door. Davey had told her about the girl and she had listened to some of what had been said.

"She asking for money?" Davey asked.

"Yeah." Ken looked at Nancy. "I don't know what to do."

"Do you think she made up that story?" Nancy asked.

"I know she did," Ken said. "But somebody did beat the living snot out of that girl."

"She said her girlfriend hit her with a telephone?" Nancy said. "Her girlfriend?"

"More likely she had somebody in one of them motels, and he beat her up and took her money. Now she's scared to go back to whoever she's with."

"You're not going to give her the money, are you?" Nancy asked.

The three of them stood, silent, and they did not look at each other.

"Nancy, hand me the cashbox," Ken said.

"You're not going to give her the money?" Nancy said.

"I'm going to give her some money." He looked into the cashbox and took out a ten and a five. He held them together, then put back the five and took out another ten. He shut the cashbox and walked out to the counter.

She was standing in the same spot, shaking. He held out the twenty dollars to her. "Here." She took it from him.

"But I need thirty dollars for a room –"

Ken found he was suddenly yelling. "I don't have to give you nothing! Now take that and get out of here!"

"Fuck you!" she screamed, but she left, and she was about to cry as she did.

Ken watched her walk down Starita Road toward the shop next to his. The further she walked, the more aware he became that he'd acted poorly. He felt a strong, sudden need to tell someone about this. He thought about his wife, his preacher, his daughter. He could think of no one he could tell.

A while later Ken saw her leave the shop next door. She walked back down Statesville Road toward Statesville Avenue, where the interstates crossed and the city limits began.

He looked at his watch. It was a quarter till noon. Traffic would be heavy that way.

Baptists on the Edge

Jim Adams always sat high in the bleachers.

When he was just Jamie Adams, a freshman at Mineral Springs High School, he went to the big basketball game against Reynolds. Reynolds was the big white high school in Winston-Salem. Mineral Springs was a little no-account white school out in the county. The game was close. In the second half a boy from Reynolds and a boy from Mineral Springs chased after a loose ball. The boy from Mineral Springs fell to the floor and pulled the Reynolds boy down with him. They were in front of the Reynolds bench. When the Mineral Springs boy tried to stand a boy from the Reynolds bench pushed him back down.

At the other end of the row of bleachers in the gym beside the church way out west on Tuckaseegee Road, the Paw Creek Baptists shouted, begging their boys, any one of their boys, to stop him. They took enough in their days, and did not want to take this, as well.

But three times their boys brought the ball upcourt, and three times they tried to run their set play, and three times Luke Adams was there where he had not been, smack in the passing lane.

The game was at Mineral Springs, out in the county, out on the mill-town edge, out beyond even the black part of town. As the boy hit the court on his back every boy and man in both stands stood up and waited. The Mineral Springs boy showed a good raising and jumped up and lunged into half the players on the Reynolds bench. The Reynolds boys scattered and swarmed around him and everybody in the gym saw one of them throw a punch.

They would see him for a moment, slowing, eyes and big hands wide, and then they would not see him speed up, and then they would see him ten feet beyond everyone else, loping and dribbling and pulling away. Before he was, they would imagine him in the air, suddenly, as if thrown, as if angry, but his right hand would reach just above the rim and he would just let go of the ball, and the net barely moved.

From both stands every boy and man poured onto the court. Jamie Adams moved with everyone else from Mineral Springs, but he stumbled from one bleacher to the next and was pushed aside, and he fell but he rolled quickly and crawled forward down the bleachers until he was on the tile. As he had fallen he had seen one of his friends, Donnie Kennedy, fall, but Donnie didn't roll and he didn't keep moving and Jamie could hear Donnie screaming for help behind him.

Luke Adams did not look at anyone shouting, for or against him, as he ran back upcourt. He made sure not to look at his father sitting high in the bleachers or at his coach clapping on the bench. He looked at his teammates to make sure they were where they were supposed to be. He looked at the other team as they brought the ball upcourt.

He crawled stumbling forward on all fours until he could get his feet underneath him. But then as soon as he could run he had to stop. The crowd surrounding the fight was so large that there was nobody near to fight. Three or four Mineral Springs boys would flank the crowd and the Reynolds bench and start punching the Reynolds boys or men just behind the fight, and their fights would stumble into corners of the gym, and men and boys would rush over to them. Mineral Springs boys at the back of a fight, with no rich kids from the city to punch, would shove those in front of them so they could get closer to the fight. As men and boys got tired of being shoved they began to shove back, and shout, and men and boys who went to the same school or job or church threw their punches at each other and whoever was close by.

They passed the ball away from Luke, worked it down into the low post where their forward spun roughly and put up a shot. The ball bounced off the backboard, clanked twice against the rim and rolled off. Their six-five center shuffled and pushed his way around the paint behind the movement of the ball. As it fell he jumped with both arms up and as he jumped he saw the yellow jersey. He tried not to look but he knew it was coming hard; without knowing, he could hear, or feel against his skin, the change in the air in the gym. He stretched and tensed and opened his hands, but then the ball stopped falling and he heard the smack and ping of other hands clapping against it, and he felt not a crash from the other body in the air, but he was falling and one side felt warm and when he landed he fell out of bounds.

Luke Adams held the ball for a second, ducked and dribbled and moved into open court.

Jamie really knew then that he was only fourteen, and he really knew then how skinny he was. Men and boys fighting someone else crashed against him, and he gave in to keep his balance and then shoved as hard as he could to get them off. He was taken up by the shirt collar and he punched twice as hard as he could and he was let go, and he was about to be punched but was knocked out of the way by somebody else's piece of the fight. He was looking for a way out when he was grabbed from behind and jerked off his feet.

Eight boys sprinted from one end of the court to the other. Luke walked, dribbling on the far side of the time line, and the Paw Creek point guard moved in front of him. With his left hand Luke dribbled to his left; he sped up as he approached mid-court. When his man was running backwards Luke crossed over and ran past him to the right. He crossed the timeline as the point guard recovered and ran at him. Luke stopped suddenly. The point guard fell past and slapped Luke's arm. Luke looked up at the ref. The ref stared back.

The point guard slowed and turned and moved in front of Luke. Luke slowly dribbled and walked along the three-point line and then threw the ball hard past the point guard's head and into the hands of his forward, rolling across the lane. Without having to dribble the forward laid it in.

Once and suddenly he spat air until his lungs were empty. His head rang and he felt inside his body the immobility of the cinder-block wall.

He saw a boy, a senior, on the football team, huge, the starter at left guard, where he himself was just a desperate third-string. With one hand he held Jamie against the wall. Jamie's hands just hung.

He was speaking. "Stay there, Jamie," he was saying.

"He traveled, ref! That was a travel, number 23!"

Jim Adams looked down at the pastor of Paw Creek Baptist Church, sitting front row in his own gym.

"He's holdin' now, ref! You ain't gonna get away with that all night, number 23!

"Don't you let that boy do that to you, Curtis!" The preacher yelled at his own son now. "You teach that boy he can't do like that to y'all. You do what you gotta do!"

"Can't nobody hit you from behind there."

He let Jamie go, and turned, and tossed and punched men and boys out of his way.

Jamie stood still. He recognized, barely, the voices that hollered or screamed around him, and he knew the faces that bled and the bodies that fell to the floor.

Soon the deputies ran in.

From the other end of the bleachers Jim Adams watched their faces twist, and listened to their rough hollers about his son. He hollered some, too, deep hollers of his own, since the Baptists with whom he now sat here in Charlotte could only scream and shout. Jim Adams always sat high in the bleachers, where he could see as much of the crowd as he could, where his back was as close to the wall as he could get it.

The Paw Creek Baptists hollered when number 23 swatted the ball from Russell Carr. Russell had been Paw Creek Baptist's best player since he was a boy, had grown up just over in the old mill village and had grown up to be six-foot-five. He had played and started for the high school last year but this year the school board said his grades weren't good enough. This number 23 for Providence Road was tall, but he wasn't that tall, and he was blond-headed and skinny and smooth-faced, and they had seen him ride up in that little red Honda Prelude his friend drove.

In the regular season their boys beat Providence Road bad. Number 23 got thrown out of the game in the third quarter when the ref turned to him, right in front of the Paw Creek bench, and said, "I've had about enough of your lip, number 23." And that number 23 boy said back, "I don't give a damn what you've had enough of."

Luke blocked the shot and the ball flew out to the key, where Providence Road's point guard caught it and raced downcourt. The Paw Creek point darted in front of him, swiping, and the Providence Road point lost the dribble and the ball rolled away. He chased and the other point chased but the Paw Creek wing got to it first, and came away onto the near side and baseballed it into the paint where Russell Carr waited under the basket, but number 23 ran through the passing lane with one arm out and pushed the ball ahead of him and turned and was ahead of everyone just past midcourt.

The Paw Creek point came up behind him and Luke crossed-over and stutter-stepped and sprinted past him, and the Paw Creek forward caught up to him and tried to lean into him but Luke went behind his back at the top of the key and drove hard. Luke jumped and the forward jumped but the point guard did not and Jim Adams watched the point guard.

Luke flew sideways, under the basket, and he brought the ball down and beneath the net and beneath the forward's hand and back up again and off the backboard into the goal. He was still flying sideways when the Paw Creek point guard lowered his shoulder and ran through Luke's legs. Luke barely felt the skin against skin; he felt his legs moving on their own. He felt them moving already so he moved them himself, sideways and around instead of up and over, and he spun in the air and landed, stumbled, fell, rolled onto his back and over and back onto his feet. He stood straight and stared at the Paw Creek point guard.

While Luke fell, the crowd, except for some of the women, had been silent, except for the gasps of those women. Men in the bleachers and the boys on the benches had stood up to see. Jim Adams could see from where he sat.

While Luke stumbled and rolled on the floor most of the Providence Road parents and all the Providence Road players had begun screaming. Some of the players on the bench had yelled for a foul call, but one boy, who wore his hair in a mullet and kept a small chain around his neck, and was not liked much by the rest of the boys, had begun to holler, from the second Luke landed safely, "Look at my man! That man got skills! God, that man is good!" and soon the rest of the players on the bench had started yelling with him.

Most of the Providence Road mothers and fathers, clustered together in the corner closest to the door, screamed for a foul call. In front of Jim Adams a big man come straight from the office in his gray suit, shouted, putting the referee and the boys from Paw Creek Baptist in their place. Jim glared at the bald spot above the gray suit and crossed his arms. If Jim had known his place he'd be on the other side of the gym, and his son would play for Paw Creek, and Providence Road would lose again. Like the fear of too little to eat, like the tension of not knowing where the next blow would come from, all the old resentments were like a layer of Jim Adams's skin, no matter the house he lived in nor the schools where he sent his children. The big man's wife finally tugged, four times, on his jacket. As he sat down Jim heard him mumble something about goddamn rednecks and ask who they thought they were. Jim thought about a quick punch to the small of his back.

The Providence Road players on the court rushed over and stood facing the Paw Creek point guard and forward, and the Paw Creek players rushed over and stood beside their teammates, and they glared at each other and talked but they all watched Luke off to the side and waited.

Luke Adams did not look at anyone shouting as he ran back upcourt. He looked up at his father sitting high in the bleachers. Neither one smiled or showed fear. The father nodded slightly. The son looked as if he might nod or even wink but he didn't. He looked at his teammates as they set up in the two-three defense. He looked at the other team as they brought the ball upcourt. Jim Adams smiled.

At a Gypsy Camping Place

Someone was banging on his door, and he woke up. Someone was yelling out in the hall, yelling his name, and he opened his eyes.

"Dowling," someone yelled. "Dowling," someone else yelled. "Chris Dowling."

"Wake up, pledge." Both of them hit the door hard. "Pledge! Pledge, get up now."

Across the hall Trotter yelled back, "Shut the fuck up," and in the hallway Tom Baity and Paul Sorriano—Chris Dowling recognized their voices now—yelled, "You shut the fuck up, dickhead."

Chris rose from his bed. His comforter fell away. He stepped into and pulled up the jeans that were lying on the floor.

"Time for war, pledge," Sorriano yelled when Chris opened the door. Chris's roommate Alex rolled over and pulled his pillow over his head. "Get dressed," Sorriano ordered.

From his closet Chris pulled his father's old camouflage hunting jacket and put it on over his shirt. He put on Gore-Tex hiking boots. He put his high school baseball cap on his head. He didn't speak.

"Hey," Baity said when Chris took his keys from his desk, "take an extra twenty with you."

"For what?" Chris asked.

"'Cause we fucking said so, pledge," Sorriano shouted. Alex groaned. "Hike up your skirt, pussy," Sorriano shouted at him.

"Trust us, man," Baity said to Chris. "You'll put it to good use."

They pushed Chris Dowling in front of them, down the hallway, down the stairs, across the courtyard and into Baity's pickup truck waiting in the fire lane. They drove in the dawn light until they were a mile or two from campus, almost out of town, until they reached the Waffle House that overlooked Highway 52. Chris recognized the cars of the other seniors in the fraternity: Sean McManus's ratty old Impala with the plastic whale on the antenna, Scott Murray's shiny red Honda Civic, Will Adams's redneck Pontiac. They ate cheaply and well, fried eggs and meats, waffles and hashbrowns, consuming the food with young men's healthy urgency even as they talked and laughed. They watched Pilot Mountain come into view as the sun burned away the dawn mist. They paid their bills and piled into the cars that had brought them, and drove north and west from Winston-Salem. They crossed the Yadkin River and crossed county lines. They drove until some would say they were in the mountains, though others would say they were just in the hills. They left the highway and chose smaller and smaller roads than ran through wider and wider fields and thicker and thicker woods. They drove up to a sign made of hand-painted plywood and turned onto a gravel lane. They parked at the lane's end, near a double-wide mobile home with a long covered porch, and a man not much older than the seniors came out to meet them and take their money.

The man directed them to the equipment they were renting for the day. Guns were distributed, along with helmets and goggles. Colors were assigned to each team, the seniors' and the pledges'. The rules were explained. The battlefield was defined by distance and feature and fence. As teams they crashed into the woods, yelling with vigor at first, war whoops and Rebel yells. Once in the woods they remembered what they were doing there; the cutthroat suburban competitiveness that got them into a good college came over their senses, and they tried to move in silence. They scattered, alone or in pairs. With a notion of hunters they tried to hide and seek, and followed, if they could, the handful of brothers who had actually hunted. Those who had hunted game walked just below the ridgelines, avoided the low ground of hollows and ravines, and tried to stick to hard ground where they'd hardly leave a print. The idea was for the teams to split to opposite barbed-wire boundaries of the paintball range, then collapse back upon each other in stealthy and haphazard combat.

Chris Dowling was alone, looking for certain landmarks, following the orders Baity and Sorriano had given him. He found what he guessed was a deer path, hard by a tree he thought was an oak, and he followed the track to a distant length of the barbed wire fence. Baity and Sorriano waited on the other side. Their paintball gear was stacked by a fence post.

"Jesus fucking Christ, pledge, we were about to go on without you," Sorriano said. "You get lost?"

"Can't you follow simple directions?" Baity asked. "Ain't you ever been in the woods before?"

"Maybe you should just go play soldier with everybody else."

"So what are we going to do, anyway?" Chris asked. "We aren't going to play paintball?"

"No. We got a better way to spend a Saturday."

"Yeah. We're lovers, not fighters."

Baity looked at Sorriano and laughed. "Dude, I don't think that came out the way you wanted it to."

"Fuck off."

They walked across the last band of forest and into a field of high brown grass.

"So your little girl back home dumped you, huh?" Sorriano asked Chris.

"Naw, she didn't dump me, man," Chris said. "We just got to talking some this summer and we, like, decided to take a break or something."

"Shit," Baity said.

"A break or something?" Sorriano said. "It's fucking November, pledge. That's not a break, that's a retirement."

"You been put out to pasture, pledge. What are you, eighteen?" Baity laughed.

"And I bet she's the only girl he's ever fucked," Sorriano said.

"How much?"

"What you got?"

"I got just enough."

"How about we bet first turn?"

"Sounds good. Come on, Dowling, be a man and win this bet for me. How many girls you fucked?"

Chris was going to lie but he waited too long to do it.

"Aww, shit," Baity yelled. "Fucking pledges."

"That, Dowling, is why you're here," Sorriano said. "We want to help you out just a bit. You need to get this little bitch back home out of your system."

They crossed the field and entered another wood. They walked down a long, slowly sloping hill and straight through a narrow stream. They climbed the rise on the other side, and when they reached the top Chris could see another opening in the woods. The space he saw was not a field but a clearing; the clearing seemed to be ringed with a perfect circle of trees and brush, and filled with some kind of long, low structures. Chris thought he heard soft music, guitars and clapping hands.

"What the fuck is that?"

Sorriano and Baity smiled. "That's the party, man," Sorriano said.

They walked into the clearing. Three mobile homes, double-wides, formed a triangle and faced each other. Dogs somewhere close by took to barking fiercely. The music stopped. They walked into the triangle. Dogs, a dozen dogs, lunged at them from beneath the mobile homes, straining against their chains and studded collars. Smoke rose in one thin column from the center of the clearing, where the ground was charred and blackened by the ashes of a campfire so big that it might have been a bonfire the night before. Two picnic tables, built of heavy two-by-fours, stood on either side of the fire pit. Two women and several men had been sitting on the picnic tables. Chris had seen them look over their shoulders and quickly leave just as the dogs began to bark. Strings of phosphorescent bulbs, the white kind used on carnival midways, hung in the air from trailer to trailer. From the corner of his eye Chris saw Baity hold up his hand, and then he saw the man on the porch.

He was not old; at least, he did not look like he should be shown deference or pity. He was older than them. His hair and beard were sandy and had been bleached by the sun to match the tan of his face. His eyes were narrow and always had been. Chris suddenly knew what the word 'wiry' really meant, and that he wasn't really wiry, he was skinny.

"Back again, gentlemen," the man said, and did not rise from his chair. Without affection he scratched the head of the black rottweiler mix at his feet. He wasn't really on a porch. He was on a wooden landing outside the door of his double-wide, which sat high above the clearing on concrete blocks. A tarp was stretched taut above him, from the roof of the mobile home to the tips of two ten-foot stakes driven into the dirt.

"Yes, sir, back again," Baity said.

"Brought you a friend," the man said, looking at Chris.

"Yes, sir, a friend of ours," Baity said.

"You going to know what to do in there, young man?" the man asked Chris.

Chris, still bewildered and more than a little scared, heard Sorriano answer, "He'll figure it out as he goes."

"I reckon he'll have to."

Baity punched Chris on the shoulder and held out his hand. After a moment Chris took the extra twenty from his wallet and put it in Baity's hand. Baity took another twenty from Sorriano and a twenty from his own wallet, and deliberately approached the man on his porch. The black dog's ears pricked up.

Baity mounted the first step only and held the bills far out. The man had to lean a little, but not much. He folded the bills carefully and slid them into his shirt pocket. Looking at the dog, he said, "Door's unlocked, gentlemen, but I ask that you knock first nonetheless."

With the back of his hand Sorriano slapped Chris in the chest. He winked at Baity and walked toward the trailer to the man's left. He knocked on the door, waited a second, and went inside.

Baity sat down on a picnic bench and started to draw in the dirt with a stick. He took a can of Kodiak from his hip pocket, put a pinch behind his lip, and offered the can to Chris, who decided right then to start.

"My grandparents live right over that way," Baity said quietly, pointing into the woods with the stick. "That's how I found out about this place. A couple of my country cousins brought me out here last Christmas."

Chris spat and spat again. The tobacco juice was filling his mouth and dribbling over his lip. He kept seeing movement on the edge of his vision, and he kept looking and he kept just missing. He could see, behind the rear tires of the pickup truck, two parallel ruts of dirt and rock that disappeared into the woods. He guessed they met some road somewhere too far away for him to see or hear. He could hear people moving among the trucks and the campers, and could see the shadows of their feet and legs from underneath the high trailer.

"They said they been coming here for a few years," Baity said, speaking of his cousins, "ever since they first showed up," meaning the man on the porch and whatever kind of tribe he led. "They said you can get pot, whatever you want here. Liquor, since the county's dry. They said they got some peyote here one time."

"Damn," Chris said. He slurped some runaway tobacco juice and spat.

"They're gone from May first, they said, all through the summer and fall. Always shows back up first of November when the fairs are done. This year my cousins called me and were like, damn, man, you need to get your ass up here and get you some of what he's brought back this year. So me and Paul tried her out last weekend. Trust me, man, she's gonna be worth the twenty dollars. We got sick of watching you moping around like a sad sack of shit. Thought this'll cure what ails you."

Tobacco juice began to overflow Chris's mouth and he spat three times. By the time the pinch was dry, so was Sorriano. He came out of the trailer with the same smile he'd gone in with. Baity stood up, said, "Wait here," and passed Sorriano halfway to the trailer door. Before Sorriano got to Chris, Baity had knocked, waited, and gone inside.

"When the fuck did you start to dip?"

Chris shrugged. "Just now, I guess."

"You guess. Fuck." For a while Sorriano just stared, shaking his head, at Chris. "That shit is nasty and it's bad for you. I order you to stop."

"It's dried out anyway," Chris said as he spat out the wad. Sorriano smiled and laughed.

The man still sat on his porch, not watching them, scratching the black dog's head. Sorriano looked at him for a minute. He seemed to wait until it was safe to speak. "You done for the season?" he asked.

"Yes I am. Last fair of the year was two weeks ago. The bounty has been harvested."

"He's a carny," Sorriano told Chris. "Look for him next time you go to the fair."

"That explains the lights," Chris said.

"Yes, sir," the man said, "I run sideshows all over the South. Go as far as Arizona and then work my way back. Got a mechanical bull in the truck. Y'all give me fifty bucks I'll set it up for you. Only ten bucks a turn."

"No, thanks," Sorriano said. "We're not here to ride bulls."

"Just watch out the bull don't ride you." The man on the porch laughed a brittle laugh, Sorriano laughed, and soon enough Chris laughed, too.

Chris looked up when he heard the door slam. Baity was coming across the clearing.

"Batter up," Sorriano said, and shoved Chris toward the trailer. Baity took a square foil wrapper from his pocket as he walked, slapped it into Chris's palm without slowing his stride, and gave him another shove in the back as they passed.

Chris knocked on the door. He waited, leaning his head. He thought he heard a faint sound inside. He looked back at the two seniors. He knocked again. He heard a voice say something softly. He opened the door and walked inside.

All the many smells of the clearing were trapped tight inside the trailer and they almost made him gag. He smelled spices and meat and smoke, bodily odors and mold. The day was bright but the trailer was dark, with heavy, brocaded curtains drawn tight across all the windows. Strung lights, smaller but the same kind as the lights outside, led along the ceiling back into the trailer's depths. A girl stood in the hall, watching him, her arms against her chest.

Chris had figured out what they were doing there. He had read about such things and knew to expect an immensely fat woman, or an old woman, or a stringy, skanky, shell of a girl. He did not expect a beautiful girl. The dark stripped her face of all but its lineaments—her cheekbones and jaw like sculpted marble, her round eyes like dark pools, her full mouth like ripening fruit. Her hands were small and fine, and her legs were thin but curved well. Chris blinked to try to see her clearly.

She lowered her arms and Chris could see the child-like waist rising to perfectly round tits. She could have come from a comic book; she could have been in a skin mag. She turned and faded into the darkness down the hall, wearing only a damp t-shirt, and Chris realized he should follow her.

He followed her to a bedroom whose walls were bare, except for a crucifix above the mattress. The mattress lay on the floor. A traveling trunk lay on the floor. The girl took off her shirt and lay down on the bed. She lay still and watched his cap, jacket and shirt fall easily to the floor. He undid his belt and his zipper. He plopped down onto the floor to take off his boots, then stood up again to take off his jeans. He stepped out of them, taking a step toward her. He stopped, reached back for the jeans, and took the condom from the pocket he'd slid it into. He rolled it onto his quickly stiffening cock.

Chris knelt until he was almost on top of her; with his skinny arms he braced himself, and began to kiss and lick her smooth brown belly. He worked his way up quickly to her tits, taking them into his mouth one by one as if he were a feasting child. He kissed each nipple. When he tired of her tits he moved up to her throat, her cheeks, and then to her mouth, and his thoughtless reflex when he saw what looked like impatience in her eyes was to go ahead and enter her.

In the silent, full-mouthed gasp of the girl on the mattress, in her pussy so tight it made his spine seize up, in the utterly exotic cocoa color and tobacco taste of her skin, Chris forgot what little he had learned on his ex-girlfriend, and in the course of the frantic pushing he forgot where he was. When he came it was a release but not a relief; he had wanted to stay inside her much, much longer.

At the far edge of the woods they retrieved their gear. Before Chris had his on, Sorriano and Baity began walking back toward the center of the battlefield. When they were ten paces ahead they turned and splattered Chris with three shots of red paint each.

On campus Chris felt as if cotton had been taken from his ears. He heard his professors more clearly and with greater understanding; his Survey of British Lit professor glowed over Chris's explication of Yeats's "Fallen Majesty," and asked if he planned to be an English major. He performed his pledge duties with alacrity, finally recited the creed without stumbling, cleaned up the house with extra polish, a few jokes, and some hustle. Sorriano and Baity gave him heaping, steaming piles of shit about it.

The leaves were finally changing color and Chris could see their brilliant light because a creature like her existed in the world. He could taste the sharpness in the coming winter air because she was out there only an hour's drive away, and he knew she was, and whenever he knew he had some time alone in his room, he jacked off slowly, to the memory of her thick dark hair, her well-made legs, her tidy breasts, the essential lines of her face.

After Hell Night and initiation, as he waited for the first of his first final exams, Chris Dowling bought a U.S.G.S. map of northwestern North Carolina. He found the paintball range in the phone book, called and asked for directons. Using the directions and the map, he circled where the trailers and the clearing had to be, highlighted the road that the ruts must lead to, and traced the route that led there from campus. He left at dawn the next morning.

The man on the porch smiled with satisfaction when he took Chris's money. "Where'd you find her?" Chris asked.

The man stopped smiling, so Chris smiled instead. "In the course of my travels," the man said.

"I just meant, like, you know, how'd you . . ."

"I did a favor for her down south," the man on the porch said slowly, after some contemplation of Chris. "She wanted to come to America.

"She's something, ain't she?"

Chris smiled at his shoes and sort of chuckled.

"Best you ever had?"

Chris smiled at the woods over his shoulder and sort of chuckled.

"That's what keeps all y'all coming back."

He thought about her more often, keeping to his study schedule but squeezing more of her in. He had only three more exams to take, then two, then one that was five days away. In waking dreams, never sleeping ones, he climbed her hill and crossed her clearing time after time after time, until at last he began to think of the clearing not as hers, but as his. He enjoyed thinking so for a little while, but that only led him back to the man on the porch, scratching the black dog at his feet. Soon Chris saw that man in his daydreams as much as he saw the girl, and when Chris made himself come he pictured her underneath that man's body, not his own, her wrists pinned to the mattress by that man's hands, her legs spread wide to receive that man.

Chris thought he might be shaking as he crossed the clearing to her door and knocked. When he had walked into the clearing this time, no one had left their seats. Dark men played guitars and watched him so closely that Chris could see the scars on their faces. Small, dark women sang and clapped their hands and kept their eyes on him. They might have been Mexicans, or they might have been Indians, or they might have really been Gypsies, or they could have once been gringos as fair and clean as Chris, but not anymore. He knocked; he heard her faraway voice and entered.

"Come with me," Chris said in her bedroom. "Uh, vaya me. Vaya me."

"Que?" she said, which Chris knew to mean "what?"

"Shh. Vaya me."

She shook her head. She did not understand. She began to take off her shirt.

"No, no. Come with me. Now. I'll take you from here and you won't have to do this anymore. You won't belong to him anymore. Come on. We can climb out your window." He moved past the foot of the bed to the wall and reached for the window latch.

"No," she said; almost screamed, in fact, and she grabbed his arm and pulled it away from the window with such force that he almost fell onto the mattress. "No, no, no, no, no," she said, almost whispered, in fact, and she stood before Chris with her hands clasped as if in prayer. She looked into his eyes and started speaking so quickly that Chris could not even recognize where one word ended and another began, much less know what she meant. She lay down on the bed, trying to pull Chris down on top of her. For a moment Chris tried to pull her up.

When he was done she was breathing hard, almost gasping. He breathed deeply and stared at her. Beneath her high cheekbones her face looked hollow; so did her eyes. Her ribs rubbed sharply against the skin below her breasts, and her skin was duller and less rich than he'd remembered, or imagined, or expected. He kissed her on the cheek.

"I will come back again soon," he said. "And then you will come with me," he said slowly. "I will get you out of this place." With what seemed like effort she rolled her head back to stare at the crucifix over the bed.

Chris dressed and stole a last glance at her, lying naked on the bed, before he left her room and opened the trailer's door. He heard the hammer lock and the dog growl, but was still about to step outside when he looked up and saw the man from the porch and his pistol staring him in the face.

"I've always been afraid of something like this," the man said, sadly and without anger. "Her being such a sweet thing and all. Always afraid some lonesome trucker, some widowed farmer, might take a bit too much of a shine to that girl." Behind the man the silent people stood gathered, staring at Chris. The man stepped back and his tribe parted, making a path Chris knew he'd have to walk.

With the pistol and the black dog close at his back, Chris Dowling crossed the clearing, away from her trailer. He strained to hear any sound that she might be making. Once he looked over his shoulder to see if he could see her at the window.

They reached the far end of the clearing and they kept walking. They walked a hundred yards and Chris looked at the woods around him. The ruts and the road were the other way, behind his left shoulder. The way he'd come the first time, the trail from the paintball range, was behind his right shoulder and getting further behind with every step. The full-on thought of what could happen slammed into Chris's mind and he finally thought to apologize.

"I'm sorry, sir. I really am. I won't come back, I swear. Believe me, sir, I will never, ever come back."

"You got that right, young man. Maybe you was doing what you thought you should, but you tried to steal another human being and that just cannot be allowed. She's the one that wanted to come to America, after all."

Chris laughed. "Yeah, you know it. I don't know what the hell I was thinking, sir. I mean, damn, I've done some stupid shit before, but, damn, this . . ."

"Aw, now, your heart was in the right place."

The woods around him were wet, the trees dripping, the ground soggy with recent rain and no sun for days. Chris felt a chill. "Sir, listen, please don't leave me out here. I have no idea where I am."

Chris made himself shut up, actually snapped his jaws together, told himself he'd be all right, that he was young and strong and could survive. He'd get through this. He'd get a good story to tell in a bar someday. He was scared but he'd get over it. He'd been dumb but he'd get a do-over. You always get a do-over, he thought. If the man had asked him about the girl right then, Chris would've had to ask what girl he meant.

"Now, because your heart was in the right place," the man said behind him, "I can't just let you go on home."

Chris thought he might piss right then, but then thought he might laugh. Goddamn, this guy is scaring me good, he thought. Maybe he just wants me to run. Maybe he just wants me to scream.

"But because your heart's in the right place," the man said, and stopped walking, "I won't make you dig your own grave."

Chris realized the man had stopped and turned around slowly to look. The man was not aiming the pistol just a little off to the side. The man's tribe had followed them into the woods. They had followed them with picks and shovels.

Chris opened his throat, but fell dead before he could truly scream.

Officially, Chris Dowling remains listed as a missing person. Neither his roommate, nor any of his fraternity brothers, knew where he might have gone after the last night he was seen on campus. Parts of his car were found in Ohio, Michigan, and even Ontario, but could not be traced back any further than a chop shop in West Virginia. Vigils were held, on campus and in the Atlanta suburb where the Dowlings lived. But whatever counseling Chris's parents sought, whatever drugs his younger brother tried, or self-degradation his sister endured, the seasons changed. Semesters and school years ended and began, children grew older, students graduated, found jobs, got married, and even the most private vigils came to an end.

Study Bible

Their high heels clicked as they crossed the tile, but stopped clicking and started scratching when they reached the carpet. Now that spring had come, they wore skirts that were not-too-short and black and not-too-tight. Their skin, which was not-too-tight either, was starting to tan from tennis-club mornings. Their jewelry clicked until they stopped in front of the information desk.

"Oh, but I was talking to Linda after garden club and …"

"Hi, may I help you?"

" … she said Eleanor never knew a thing."

"Not a thing?"

"Not a thing."

"Hm-hm-hm. Study bibles?"

"I beg your pardon?"

"Study bibles."

"Oh, okay," the bookseller said. "They're right over …"

"Yes, we need study bibles for our bible class."

"We hear it makes all the difference, having a study bible instead of just a regular bible."

"I'm sure it does," the bookseller said. "Obviously, depending on what …"

"We'll be using it for a bible study class."

"The Sarah Jenkins Simpson Fellowship class."

"Oh. Okay." They had been walking, and had reached the section for bibles, three cases of six shelves each, between Inspirational

Fiction and Islamic studies. Bibles in a Babel of sizes and colors and covers and versions—black leather-bound, burgundy leather-bound, white leather-bound, blue leather-bound, pocket-sized paperbacks, hardcover dust-jacketed, devotional bibles, devotional bibles for men, devotional bibles for women, devotional bibles for teens and bibles including the Apocrypha—were flushed and arranged spine-out on the varnished wooden shelves, and mixed in among them were the study bibles.

"Well, here are all our bibles," the bookseller—who had a name, which was Wendy—said. "What …"

"Great, now which of these are the study bibles?"

"Don't you have a section of just study bibles?"

"No, they're organized by version …"

"Which of—oh, here's one."

"Surely you have a section just for the study bibles."

"Here's one."

"Well, is that the one we want?"

"I don't know. Which of these is the best?"

Wendy asked, "Which version do you prefer?"

"We want study bibles."

"Yes, but which version …"

"Well, it's for this fellowship class."

"It's for a class at our church."

"Okay. Do you prefer the King James …"

"Oh. I like the NRSV."

"Really?"

"Oh, yes, I think it's the most mainstream."

"Do you have any study bibles in NRSV?"

"All our NRSV bibles are right here."

"I just think the Living Bible's too, I don't know, secular."

"So where are the NRSVs?"

"They're right …"

"Which are the study bibles?"

"They're mixed in with the …"

"Is there anyone here who can help us with this?"

Wendy couldn't answer immediately. She looked at the ground and scratched her chin. Her head shook slightly. She slowly said, "Ma'am, I can try to help you find one."

"Well, then, which of these is the best study bible?"

"Tell you what, ma'am, I'm going to go check our computer."

"It has to be NRSV."

"Yes, ma'am. I'm going to check our computer for all the study bibles we have in NRSV. I'll be right back." She walked away quickly, gesturing.

"My, look at all these bibles."

"Oh, here are the NRSVs."

"Oh. But where are the study bibles?"

"I don't know. Oh, here's one. They're all mixed in."

"Yes, I see one down here."

They each drew a New Revised Standard Version study bible from a shelf and thumbed through.

"I'm not sure if I like this one."

"This one's not bad."

They swapped, and thumbed again.

"Well, what do you think?"

"I don't know … oh, look at that one there." She reached and brought down a thick, hardcover bible with a beige dust jacket. Its publisher had designed the jacket to look more like that of a pseudo-academic best seller than the bible your grandfather carried to church every Sunday. She reached again and brought down another copy. Those publishers know their business.

Wendy came back. "I'm afraid we don't have many study …"

"Oh, we found this one here."

"Yes, we both like this one."

"That's the one I used in coll…"

"So do we pay up front?"

"Yes, ma'am, our registers are right …"

"Okay, great, thank you so much."

In a moment their heels were clicking across the tile.

The Lexus and the Mercedes were parked next to each other in the lot, and the two women faced each other between their cars.

"I can't wait to look into this."

"Yes, I think it will be so much more helpful than just a regular bible."

"Um-hm."

"Yes."

"Well, we will have to do this again next week, Lois."

"We certainly will, we certainly will. You take care, Peggy."

"You, too, Lois. Bye-bye now."

"Bye now."

"Bye."

Lois lowered herself into the Lexus, closed and locked the door, and turned the ignition. She put the gear shift into drive and, without checking, pulled into the lane. Nothing hit her.

She drove home, humming while the radio was on the classical music public radio station. She hummed a different tune than the one playing, which was one she did not know. She hummed the tune she had heard that morning. She was humming and faintly happy, but she was not smiling. Her lips were pressed close together as they always were when she drove. She was passed on the left and the right, and Lois thought about what a pleasant town this had been when she moved here. Crews were working on the road and she stared straight ahead and braced herself to stare straight ahead. This really was a city now, though, and that was nice; when you met people from other parts of the country you could say "Charlotte" and didn't have to add "North Carolina" when they asked you where you were from.

Her house was three elm-shaded miles away. She arrived, parked, entered, noticed but did not read a note left by the maid, sat, crossed her legs and dozed off in Genesis.

She woke before her husband came home. She set the bible on the coffee table, stood up and smoothed her skirt. She looked around the room; it was straight. With the kids grown and gone there were fewer stains and scratches on the walls, floors and furniture; there were fewer books and magazines and odds and ends lying around. She went into the kitchen.

The sun was still shining, though its shining against the elms threw long shadows across the yard, and the view from the house was already darkening. The clock on the oven showed 6:30, but she didn't worry. He always worked late. And the drive home, boy … all that traffic leaving Uptown. She didn't worry. At seven she set a pot of water to boiling and started cooking the fresh pasta the maid had bought that morning. When it was almost ready he walked in from the garage.

She turned from the table she was setting. "Hi, dear."

"Hey." He glanced around the kitchen, at the stove, the window, the maid's note and the set table, looking quickly at each as if trying to learn an unexplored room as quickly as he could, and he did this every night.

"How was your day?" Lois asked.

He nodded and set his briefcase down by the desk. He picked up the maid's note and began reading. "Fine," he said. He put the note back down.

"Dinner's ready, if you want to go ahead and eat."

"I will in just a minute."

"That's fine."

He went upstairs.

Lois emptied the pasta from the colander into a dish and ladled sauce over it. She put the dish on the table. She poured iced tea into a glass for her husband, poured red wine for herself and felt the shiver of being naughty. She took both glasses to the table, set them in their proper places, sat down and sipped the wine. She crossed one leg over the opposite knee and let it dangle in a slow meter, and stared at her husband's briefcase on the floor.

He came back and sat and she said a blessing and he ate silently, nodding occasionally as she talked.

"Peggy and I had a wonderful day today. We went over to SouthPark. We both got these wonderful study bibles for the fellowship class. I started reading it as soon as I got home. I think it will be a great help."

She took a bite of pasta, chewed precisely and swallowed. "I am looking forward to this class." She took a sip of wine. "I think we'll really get a lot out of it. And I think we'll enjoy it. Did you hear from anyone today?"

He shook his head. He swallowed. He spoke. "Not really."

"You know what Peggy told me today? Peggy told me that Eleanor Sinclair didn't know a thing about Jack until he left her. Isn't that awful? She didn't even have a clue."

He shook his head. "Hm."

"Isn't that awful?"

"Um-hm."

"Just terrible."

Lois had finished her pasta. She took her napkin from her lap and dabbed the corners of her lips, let the napkin fall into a fold around her fingers and set it beside her plate, sliding it under the edge of the plate to keep it from re-opening. She folded her hands and set them neatly on the edge of the table.

"Are you going to the meeting tonight?" she asked.

"Yes."

"Which one is it tonight?"

"Long-range planning."

"Ah, yes."

He swallowed the last bite of his pasta and threw his napkin on the table. He drank the last of his iced tea and pushed the chair away from the table.

"I'd better go get ready," he said. "I want to catch Dr. Hammond before the meeting."

"What do you need to talk to him about?"

"Some of the plans for the new capital campaign."

"The one for the prayer chapel?"

"Um-hm."

"Oh."

He took the paper upstairs with him. Lois had cleared the table when he came back down. She was drinking another glass of red wine by the window over the sink.

"I shouldn't be too late," he said.

"Okay," she said, and smiled.

"Bye."

"Bye-bye."

Lois finished the wine, set the glass in the sink and walked into the living room. She kicked off her shoes and lay down on the couch. She picked up the study bible, and decided to try the New Testament this time. She flipped between each of the Gospels, finally settling on Mark. She scanned the chapters and the verses, and began reading near the end. She fell asleep in chapter 12.

The Postpunk Chronicles

Mary McCaskill woke one evening in a trailer outside Charlotte, and decided she was through with it. She had turned her back on civil life and all its rules and comforts. She had spent more time at clubs than at her jobs. She had hung out with thugs and thieves and dealers. She had lived in city parks, sleeping on the hilltop tennis courts where she could see all around her, and had spent her days wandering around town with all she owned in a backpack. She had unimaginable freedom, had flung herself against its far walls, and now she wanted a home. She slipped out of the trailer while the others were still asleep. Scared and coming down, she walked in the dark, beside ripe fields, for close to two miles. She found a shut-down gas station with a pay phone that worked, and called her mother to come pick her up.

Two weeks later she found out she was pregnant.

Her mother got her a job at the new superchain bookstore, with the minimum wage but with excellent health benefits. She shelved her section next to a woman named Wendy, who was comforting and kind. Mary lived with various friends, sleeping on sofas and in a couple of bathtubs, and then with Derek, the baby's father, until she found him too unstable. She moved in with her mother. When the child, a son she named Finn, was born, she gave the father another chance. He blew it within a year. One night he flipped on her, calling her vile names, and then he hit her. He thought a good smack would keep her in line, and was surprised when she hit him back. He was more surprised that she hit harder than he did. She took Finn and left. A friend of hers asked, "Won't Finn need a male role model?" Mary replied, "Hell, I'm a better man than that nancy boy." Her father, a lawyer, helped her apply for a termination of parental rights. Derek was informed but he did not contest. Mary was raising Finn on her own when Wendy introduced her to Will Adams.

Will Adams had left graduate school disgusted with the cloistered thing he'd become. He left after a year-and-a-half of coursework, without his master's degree or any practical skill. His slow mastery of English meters and his deep readings of Joyce and Saint Augustine did not hold up in the marketplace.

He thought about moving north to the capital, straining if not breaking his ties. In the end he moved back to Charlotte, even though his father had told him that he couldn't live at home. Jim Adams was furious, and threatened Will with everything from predictions of a dire future to a good old-fashioned ass-whipping. Will's father wanted a professor in the family. He wanted for his son an outward and visible sign of enlightenment and achievement, with a steady paycheck. He had long since decided that Will was too gentle for any of the more strenuous professions. He reminded Will that the only 40-hour-a-week job he had ever had was delivering truck parts for him, and then just for the summers he was home from college. Will found a job driving the parts truck for Ken Murphy at Brake & Clutch Service, one of his father's competitors.

He found Wendy, who was renting out a room. Every morning Will hid a small tape recorder and blank sheets of paper in his hip pocket. All day he drove industrial streets, composing onto the tapes. When he had to, and could, he pulled over and made notes on the paper. Each night he sat in Landmark or Athens or some other all-night diner and wrote quickly into notebooks. He tore out full sheets, re-wrote his drafts onto fresh sheets, cleaned. He would go to his rented room and type; after she got to know him, Wendy let him use her computer. When he finished they'd drink beer together and talk. She had been a wild child, had tried a variety of drugs, and had married fairly young. She was divorced now. She had children who weren't there, though their pictures were, and months passed before she told Will that one was institutionalized and the other had died as a toddler, after a long illness. Will had nothing to say to that; if he had, he probably wouldn't have remembered what Wendy told him. Wendy started taking him to the bars and clubs he'd have never found himself, the places where the unusual bands played; slowly, the monkish reclusion in which he'd wrapped himself for years began to fall away. Wendy introduced him to people. She introduced him to Mary McCaskill.

Mary and Will began dating. She liked his eyes, and the faint scars beside the left one that made him look like he'd been around a bit. They were just hanging out and fucking, really, until Jesus's funeral. Mary had a friend she had lived with in the parks who had been convinced that he was Jesus Christ, the Messiah come again. If you denied him he would smile gently and gently argue, until you stopped or became angry. If you became angry he would stop, and his eyes would fill with forgiveness. He was living among his people, preparing himself until his time came. He wandered the nation, appearing once on the front page of *The Washington Post*, in a picture accompanying an article about street kids in New Orleans. They listed "Jesus" as his "street name," like "Spike" or "Spider." Years later he came back to Charlotte, and went riding in the car of a silly girl who'd drunk a 12-pack that night. As the car flipped down an embankment he was thrown out, and smashed his head against a tree.

At the memorial service his friends were either lined in a crescent behind the funeral home, or lining the walls of the room where the open casket lay. His skateboard had been placed in his arms, and someone had convinced the funeral home to play a Siouxsie and the Banshees tape. Two scraggly boys held each other, sitting on the floor to the side of the casket, crying uncontrollably. The family and their friends, thick and calloused and tired, wearing clean trousers and their best shirts, familiar with each other and with these services, filled the hallways and the parlor. Will went with Mary, standing behind her while she comforted friends she hadn't seen in years. After they left he rode with her silently while she drove out to the western edge of the county, where she had grown up, and sat with her by the river while she cried.

Mary by now had stopped shaving her head, and was even growing it long. For years Will had started every morning with push-ups and sit-ups. His buddy Ben brought him along to his gym. Ben was working at Brake & Clutch while he waited for a spot to open in the fire department. All that, and age, and the constant lifting of his job began to thicken Will's narrow frame. He began to look like his father. He fought a few fights, had a pistol pulled on him once outside a redneck bar called the Rock Porch, and began to feel better about himself. Will moved out of Wendy's room and into Mary's apartment. After several months they realized that they'd never had an argument, in part because they recognized that between the two of them such a thing would be fearsome to behold, but mostly because they complemented one another well. Mary was making herself safer, and Will was making himself more dangerous. They could stand up to each other.

Will submitted his poems to magazines that rejected them often and impersonally, until they began rejecting them with words of encouragement. He suddenly, and for the first time, thought about making more money. When the warehouse manager at the shop retired, Will applied for and got the job. He married Mary and adopted Finn, who couldn't remember Derek. Will had taught him to throw a football, and had told him the story of Huck Finn. A magazine published one of Will's poems; a well-known magazine published three. Mary found a receptionist job at the law firm of a friend of her father's, and found a few dresses that covered her tattoos. Will sold the bank stock his grandfather had given him as a child. He made a down payment on a house, an arts-and-crafts bungalow in what had been one of Charlotte's first suburbs, then a slum; plaques now called it a historic district. A month before the millennium ended, Will and Mary had a daughter they named Juliet.

One night, not two years after Juliet was born, Mary Adams found herself sitting quietly at a poetry reading where neither she nor Will wanted to be. She found herself unable to comment or leave when she heard Steve Quinn say that while he worked on his master's degree at Columbia, he lived in a basement apartment up in the 130s, "where all the junkies hung out."

"All of them?" Mary wanted badly to ask.

"They were always real cool to me, though," Quinn said. "They wouldn't hit me up for change 'cause they knew I didn't have any money, but I'd read 'em poems every morning on my way to class. My poetry isn't exactly to everyone's taste. I've got sort of a reputation, I guess, as kind of a punk-rock poet. Which is cool. I am, of course, very influenced by that music and by the, the whole scene, and the attitude, the, the, the, the freedom of punk rock. That's part of our heritage, too, you know.

"I worked for years on this next poem. This one's for the junkies. What I wanted to do was communicate some absolute, stripped-down, raw life. I wanted there to be an uninterrupted line from my soul to the page. And that, to me, is very, very punk rock."

Mary wanted very badly to say, "No, actually, no the fuck it's not." Then she wanted to stand up and call him a poser, a tourist. Steve Quinn was a visiting adjunct professor of English at the state university north of town, and Black Fox Books had just published his first chapbook of poems. He was building a reputation as a dangerous young poet. The university was proud to have him; they thought his hiring showed dash. They were starting their own literary press. They needed a poetry editor. Will wanted to be that poetry editor. Mary kept her mouth shut.

Will had suddenly and recently felt too old for the Joe Strummer anti-status of his job. For the first time since he was in graduate school he thought about effect and position within a community. When the university announced they'd received a grant to found a press, the school's poet-in-residence told Will he should apply to be their poetry editor; after one slow shift in the warehouse, he did. He and Mary had a long talk about it, because editing poetry would pay less than managing the warehouse did. "This is something I could do for the rest of my life, though," Will said. "I'd make good contacts." He was sad as he said this; so was Mary, even though she agreed and encouraged him. He submitted his resume, with photocopies of his published work attached, and he went to interview with the press's director. Will had qualifications: a sizeable chunk of education from a prestigious university, the publication of his own work in widely respected magazines and in one soon-to-be-published anthology. He was definitely in the running. He would know their decision by the end of the month. Was he coming to the faculty reading on Saturday the 21st?

"Um, yes, I've been looking forward to it," Will said. He and Mary found a babysitter, and Mary found herself sitting quietly, politely.

After the reading, after the fetes and the serious questions, while Will talked to the director of the press, Mary spoke in the ear of the poet-in-residence who was, in some small way, responsible for her being there. "If I had to sit through this," she told him, "and Will doesn't get this job, I'm going to kick your ass. You know that, right?"

Christopher Terrell smiled at her. "I have no doubt. Glad to hear you haven't gone completely respectable on me." Christopher Dante Terrell had grown up on the same west side as Mary and had gone to the same high school, where the full extent and nature of his and Mary's friendship had been crudely and sometimes violently discussed. Because he was a black man who had gone to West Mecklenburg High and had lived in New York City, Charlotteans thought Christopher had an edge, a toughness, a glamour of danger, and to a degree he did. That degree, however, was due solely to something inside Christopher himself, who had grown up as comfortably as Will Adams had. Christopher's father was a successful builder. Christopher was a Morehead Scholar, a holder of impressive degrees from UNC and Columbia, and a nationally praised poet. He wasn't sure, but he seemed to recall that it was sometime after the Rodney King riots, when he was a freshman at Chapel Hill, that every young black man was now thought to come from Compton or someplace that must be very much like it. White students were surprised to see him in classical studies classes, and, once they got over their nervousness, were unstinting and unthinking with their praise and encouragement. That made him an angry young black man. After graduation he left North Carolina, the state and the university, and worked on his MFA at Columbia, living, glory Hallelujah, in New York City. Christopher thought he'd never return to Charlotte. He carved himself a place in the ongoing frontier of the millenial city, where the density, the unknowable multiplicity, allowed for vast projects of self-invention. After classes he burrowed just a few feet underground, renaming himself Hoss Civitas, winning prizes and renown in the poetry slams and spoken-word concerts of lower Manhattan and Brooklyn. He moved to Williamsburg, had a view of the river and a string of impressive girlfriends.

Christopher was shocked when his father had his stroke. He was shocked to see his father helpless and weak in the hospital, he was shocked to find himself wanting to be near his family, he was shocked that he wanted to leave all he was shaping in New York and come back to Charlotte. That the university, which had started as a GI Bill commuter school and was striving for respectability and regard, needed a poet-in-residence was pointed out, to the board of trustees and to Christopher.

As much as Christopher wanted to stay cool, to write and teach and leave it at that, he began to build a community around himself. He built it up out of faculty readings and coffeehouse readings and student slams, of making sure poetry played a part in the downtown arts, of writing guest columns for the newspaper and commentating on public radio. He found, on the faculties of the university and the other three colleges in town, on the staffs of the local bookstores, and in certain corners of the west side where most people would not know to look, young writers with energy and skill. He found none that matched his skill, though, his reach across empires and years, until he and Will Adams met. They heard each other read and eyed each other warily; they talked and made each other nervous. When Christopher saw Mary McCaskill at an open mike one night, he thought at first she was there to see him. He and Will tested each other, respected each other, and tried to get along. Christopher honestly thought Will was the best possible poetry editor the new press could have, and without reservation he told the director so.

When Will got the job he and Mary were happy. Mary knew Will wanted, and deserved, a greater place both in the community Christopher had built and in the city itself, a place from where he could offer and affect. For Christ's sake, though, the radio in their kitchen stayed tuned now to National Public Radio. How in the hell had that happened, Mary asked herself. They were visiting a Methodist church, where the pastor smiled too placidly and too much, and spoke to make it seem too damn easy, as if something easier than love would do, or as if love wasn't the hardest thing in the world. Will hung his blue jeans and his work shirts in the closet, and bought a couple of blazers. The law firm gave Mary more responsibilties and she handled them responsibly, until she was doing the work of a paralegal and making a paralegal's pay. She was working diligently at her desk one afternoon when Derek startled her by walking in. She did not shudder or flinch, of course. She stared at him coolly while he said hey, and she did not speak.

"I need to talk to a lawyer," he said. He had taken out a couple of piercings, and had grown a bushy, patchy beard.

"For what?"

"I want to file a religious discrimination suit against my boss."

What in the hell, she thought. "We don't do that here," she said.

"Naw, come on, I need to sue. My boss says I got to shave my beard off. He says the customers don't like it."

"What are you doing, delivering pizzas?"

"Yeah."

Holy shit.

"I can't cut my beard, it's against my religion."

Asking, 'what kind of sorry-ass religion are you and your loser friends into now?' would only prolong the conversation. "We don't do religious discrimination."

"Do you know anybody who does?"

"No."

"You're looking good these days."

"Fuck off." She didn't need him to tell her she looked good. Her auburn hair was shoulder-length and auburn again, with subtle streaks of fire-engine red. She favored long skirts that showed off her hips.

"No, I mean it, you look good. You look all professional and shit. I remember you walking around town in those cut-off jeans all the time, people driving by all staring at your tattoos. You were the coolest girl in this shitty little town. Come on, you don't need to be so mean."

"I'm mean 'cause I want to be. Fuck off."

"You going to see Revvenint tomorrow night?"

"Fuck off."

"Mary, come on."

"Why haven't you fucked off yet?" She picked up her phone and began to dial.

"What, you going to call the cops on me? I ain't done nothing. Go ahead and call the fucking cops on me."

"I'm not calling the cops. I'm calling my husband." Mary smiled at him.

Will had never seen Derek, but Derek had seen him, and Derek had heard that Will had said, before he married Mary, that if Derek ever looked at Mary or Finn again he, Will, would pound on his, Derek's, face until it came out of his ass.

Derek sputtered, trying to say something cool as he walked quickly out the door. "So call your fucking husband, bitch. I ain't scared of . . ."

"Hello?"

"Hey, babe," Mary said. She looked up, and the office door was swinging shut.

"Hey. What's up?"

"Nothing," Mary said. Why send Will to the Revvenint show already looking for a fight? "I just wanted to call and say hey."

Hell, yes, she was going to the Revvenint show. She would feel like she was taking off a costume, letting her office dress fall to the floor, pulling on jeans and her combat boots. Will would put his slacks and jacket in the closet, and wear the kind of clothes he'd worn when they were dating. No pussy like Derek could keep her away. Long before the newspaper and the alternative newspaper saw fit to run a notice, word had spread: Revvenint would play again. They were heroes in Charlotte, the first hometown punk band to be heard of outside the Carolinas. Their Halloween shows were the stuff of legend, with the lead singer coming out on stage with his head inside a jack-o-lantern, which the guitarist would remove by smashing it with a shovel. Now they were almost retired and upstanding; the guitarist had run twice for city council in one of Charlotte's satellite towns. Charlotte itself could still act like a town, and word spread quickly through certain of its sides. If you knew, you knew who to tell. Well-armed Timmy Newman, who'd settled into a job as a bounty hunter for the bail bondsman across the hall from Mary's office, told Mary. He had a friend who knew a couple of the guys in the band, and he knew that Mary had known the guys in the band back in the day, back in the days when they all hung out at the Pterodactyl Club. Mary knew who to tell.

Without a word on TV or the radio, word spread, throughout the mill town watershed, as far north as Winston-Salem, as far south as Columbia. The word reached up the creeks and forks, into west Mecklenburg, Cornelius, Derita, and Concord. The word crossed the Catawba on its way to Belmont, Gastonia, Lincolnton, and Shelby. They could count on crews to come down from Mooresville and Statesville. By the day of the show Mary knew that all her old friends, the ones she never got to see much anymore, would be there.

The show was in an abandoned warehouse that had become a music hall. For years after its conversion the place was obscurely known at best, standing a couple of long, dark blocks off the serious thoroughfares, in the borderlands of neglect. At first it took some guts to go there. Charlotte's money kept seeping, though, and now the music hall stood in a capital-D District, both Entertainment and Historic, and after so many years in such a New South city, the place was now positively venerable. The ticket booth was just inside the old primary loading dock, the bar was just beyond it, the bathrooms just past the door on the left. Sofas and chairs were scattered to the right, along with a couple of pool tables and a plywood partition that marked off what they called backstage. The building was shaped like an L; the long arm of the warehouse that ran beside the loading dock was where the bands played. Risers and wires and speakers lurked along its far wall. Bare benches stretched along the opposite wall, on either side of the barricaded soundboard. Will and Mary and Mary's friends sat on one of the benches, drinking beer before the band started.

"Where are the kids?" Glenn asked.

"Safely in the suburbs," Mary said. "Spending the night with my dad."

"You should have brought them," Glenn said, quarter-joking at most. His parents had never been around much when he was growing up, so he was big on family togetherness. His father was an Outlaw biker; his mom got messed up on cocaine. His back against the wall, Glenn appeared to ignore the sullen, pretty girl who spoke seriously in his ear. With small movements his eyes took in the whole of the room, and a good bit of what was outside. He once had been a skinhead. Growing up when and where he did, he saw no reason not to see the world as a battleground for tribes, or to see west-side white kids like him and Mary as soldiers on a front line. On those rare days when he showed up at high school, he always sat for lunch at the popular kids' table, claiming his seat before they got there. By himself he displaced the in-crowd, turned them into refugees. He was stared at, grumbled about, but never asked to move, never even approached. Mary would walk up smiling and say, "Is this seat taken?"

"Yeah," Glenn would snarl, "by a smart-ass red-headed punk-rock girl. Sit the fuck down."

Glenn owned his own tattoo shop now, and made a good living

at it. He'd given Mary several of her tattoos. A football player once beat up Mary outside the school, because she was a freak, and because he could get away with it because she was a freak. He thought. Glenn tracked the guy down and beat him to the ground outside his own house.

Mary drank her beer and looked around. She saw a lot of her friends here tonight. Her friends, the ones who hadn't truly fucked up or flamed out, understood the deal. You placed a price on freedom or safety, self-respect or comfort. You placed a price on your wildness. Nobody had the cash to pay for them all at the same time. You want freedom? How much do you want and how bad do you want it? How much safety are you willing to trade for real freedom, how much comfort for not hating what you saw in the mirror? She and her friends had no truck with that hippie shit about peace and harmony, because anyone with sense and experience knows there are some evil motherfuckers out there who will take from you whatever they can. You can't have your pot and smoke it, too. Her friends knew the rules and knew the need for them. If they didn't want to obey one or more of them, fine, but they were ready and willing to pay the price. If your boss wanted you to shave, you shaved, or you quit, or you shrugged when he fired you. You sure as hell didn't sue. The losers who called for Anarchy Now! were the ones who'd least be able to survive it.

Dave and Maggie were in the corner; they'd hung out with Mary at the Pterodactyl Club, almost every night of the early 1990s. Dave was a stonemason with his own company now; Maggie had gone back to school. Debbie and Ginny from high school were talking in the lobby. Billy Dell and some buddies were standing near the stage. Billy got out of prison not long ago, found a job at Hager's Garage, and was studying to get his technical degree. On the way in she had seen Kristin and Paul and Sally, and plenty of faces she'd been seeing for years.

But most of the faces she saw inside she did not know, and they did not know her. They seemed, sweet Jesus, like kids to her. They had been warned to stay away. The music writer for one of the papers had told them not to come tonight, if their idea of punk was a band with numbers in their name. Some, she was sure, were as honest and fearless as she had been. Most, though, looked like children out slumming, confusing stupid with wild, fucked-up with rebellious, and always ready to slip back south to the suburbs as soon as it got unsafe. They looked like the kids she always saw huddling in the mall, cruising the shops where they could buy their look. When she was their age she and her friends got run out of the mall because of how they looked.

When punk hit Charlotte there were a dozen, maybe two dozen of them, spread thinly all over town. They were, or at least they felt like, rejects in one way or another. Most of them were working-class kids, not quite poor but close. For whatever reasons of taste, set of mind, or preference, they were not drawn to the other musics and means of identity available in their parts of the city: heavy metal, glam, country, the hip-hop culture that was just being born. Mary herself wasn't poor; her father was a lawyer, the first in his family to get out of the mills, but he chose to live on the far west side, closer to Gastonia than Charlotte. Mary's mother had left her father when she was six. When Mary was 13 her mother took her to Washington, DC, and took her shopping in Georgetown. On M Street she saw her first punks, loitering with their Mohawks and leather and chains. For the first time she saw a scene she'd be happy to join, a uniform she wouldn't mind wearing. She saw a way to fuck up the suburbs. The other Charlotte kids who'd somehow found punk found each other quickly, over three or four years, and carved out parts of the city as theirs. They made places where they could almost feel like they belonged. See what has become of it, she thought. Unless you were willing to take one dare after another until one of them finally killed you, then sooner or later life would roll up on you, grim and superficial, a heavy march of work weeks and seasons.

At last the man in the shiny coat came out on stage, screaming like a wrestling announcer, like a televangelist. Those who once were spread around the hall now swarmed to the front of the stage—fierce, eager supplicants. The man in the shiny coat asked if they were ready, really and truly ready. Or did they just think they were? He posed them other challenges. With a big smile he questioned their fitness, their worthiness, their ability to withstand the attack they were about to face. The answers rose from whoops and hollers to a sustained and swelling yell, kept up so loud and so long that it became a background hum that only a shout through six-foot speakers could break. Frantic himself, the man in the shiny coat introduced the band and got the hell out of the way.

Pounding, blasting, punching, Revvenint played its first song while the crowd before them leapt, hopped, shook. From the high ceiling behind the stage a banner dropped: a double-barreled shotgun, both hammers cocked and aimed straight at the crowd. The crowd ate it up, yelled louder. A wide half-circle in front of the stage became a pit: young guys shirtless and already sweating, big guys who looked like they'd come down out of deep hills for this. They wore only overalls and work boots and long, bushy beards. Maybe they wore a CAT or John Deere hat, but that was all right because they looked like they could drive a CAT or a John Deere. Those corn-fed country boys got to heaving their bulks and the shirtless guys scattered, thrilled, and rushed back harder into the pit. Even Mary and Glenn and Will stayed out of that pit, and stood instead just behind it, working up a good sweat song by burst of song.

The singer went off stage once. He came back carrying an eight-foot folding table. The pit cleared back as he set up the table in front of the stage. He grabbed a bag full of beer bottles and smashed it once, twice, on the floor, and they cheered him on as he spread the broken glass across the tabletop. They let loose Rebel yells as he climbed back on stage and they hollered like the devil as he belly-flopped onto the table, as it collapsed beneath him, as the shattered glass skidded across the concrete floor into the crowd. Guys jumped onto the shards of glass and rolled around in them. The singer climbed back on stage bleeding badly, as the crew strung barbed wire around the edge of the risers.

Mary watched the pit with a benedictory smile. Will had told her about villages in Scotland and England where, for as long as anyone could remember, they celebrated certain holy days or some victory over the Vikings by playing an ancient game that let them beat the holy shit out of each other. Half the population would try to carry a ball (in the beginning it had been a head) from one end of town to the other, while the other half bloodied them and themselves senseless trying to stop them. Will told her about the endless wars and raids on the Borders, and the wicked ballads sung on either side of the frontier. He told her about all the many migrations, across the sea, into the hills and valleys, out of the mountains, into the mills. They adapted and even prospered. Most of them went soft, one way or another, one generation to the next. Relatively, they all prospered as the country did, as the South did, as Charlotte did: none of them came up as hard as their parents and grandparents had. They had lost the ballads, but something remained, and it begged for battle.

In time, Glenn went back to the wall and the sullen girl who was waiting for him. Will went to the bar to buy two more beers. In front of the stage the punks thrashed about, pummeling themselves on each other. They jumped heavily, with force. The pit moved slightly at its edges, to the left, to the right, up and back. Inside the pit two or three guys might start moving in time together, back and forth, threatening to act like a wave. If they did, though, somebody would bust them up in a hurry. Somebody'd come slamming into their harmony from the side, crossways, and send them spinning back into rugged individualism. Some guys swung their arms. Some guys used their shoulders. Guys would go down and get piled on. Guys bled and roared and had a good time. Behind the pit more punks danced, hollered, jumped in place. Mary occupied a space for two while Will was gone to the bar.

She was falling forward before she understood that she'd been shoved. She put her hands up, and caught herself against some backs in front of her. She thought at first that Will might be trying to be funny, but she did not see him over her shoulder. People got shoved and worse at Revvenint shows; she thought nothing of it. She was jumping in place when she was shoved again, again from behind, while she was in the air. From the ground she looked up but not behind her, and she saw Derek disappear into the crowd. She stood up with her fists at her sides. She looked for Will in the back of the room; she looked for Glenn in the place he'd been sitting. She told herself she should get out of the crowd, get her back to the wall. She stayed in place, looking all around her. She looked around for Derek.

She heard a cry and turned in time to see two or three teenage girls falling on top of her, and she saw Derek standing behind them. She stood her ground against the weight of their slight and dainty forms. She shoved them back at Derek, but he was gone. She looked through the crowd. She caught a glimpse of his beard but lost it. Eager and getting angry, she checked all the angles, and started slowly making her way out of the crowd and toward the wall.

She felt a tap on her shoulder and spun, her left arm raised to block and her right cocked back to punch. She was facing some guy she didn't know. He jerked his head and thumb towards the side of the stage. The guy had seen what was happening, and had seen Derek, who was keeping his head low like a little boy playing soldier. Now Mary saw Derek, too, and when he slid between a dancing couple Mary slid herself, sideways and towards him, and stuck her leg out. Derek met her leg with his shins, and his foot didn't move forward like he wanted it to. He pitched forward, flailing, and fell into the heart of the pit. Buffetted, he began to scream, and then to cuss weakly, and then to plead. Mary turned her back and walked toward the back of the hall.

At the End of Ocean Boulevard

On Ocean Boulevard, behind the wheel of his truck, with his wife beside him, and her best friend beside her, Ben Cooper recalled how excited his father had been when he'd told him where they were staying.

"Y'all are staying in Ocean Drive," his father had shouted. "Hot damn, I used to have me a time down there. Whoo."

"I didn't say Ocean Drive, Dad," Ben had said. "I said Ocean Boulevard. Our condo's almost at the end of it. Out past Cherry Grove."

"Boy, I started going to Ocean Drive soon as I was old enough to look at a pretty girl," Ben's father had gone on. "We'd catch a ride down there every chance we got." He had stood up and walked across his little plank porch. "That was a hot time, I tell you." He had poured more Fighting Cock into his jelly jar, completed the glass with ginger ale, and stirred with his finger. "When y'all leaving?"

"Friday, after this next shift ends."

"Y'all all piling into one car?"

"No. I'm taking Lucas and Debra's mama on down Friday morning. Debra's coming down after work with her friend Ginny."

"Why y'all doing that?"

"Because Debra can't get off till five. I'm done in the morning, and I got to be back Sunday for my next rotation, so I want to go on and get down there."

His father had grunted, squinting at his son from the corner of his bloodshot eye. "You ever been down to Myrtle before?"

"Yeah."

"When you go?"

"Few years ago. Went with some guys from the station."

"You did?"

"Yeah."

"Your little brother used to go down there all the time. Big deal, as I recall, him and his buddies'd always go down that first week they's out of school. What they call it?"

"First Week."

"That's her. You never went to that."

"Nah."

"You always had you a job soon as school ended."

"Yeah."

"I know your mama must've appreciated that."

His father, grinning, had bared his crooked, yellow teeth.

"I guess she did," Ben had said to him. His father had shook his head, still smiling.

"Well, I'd of hoped she'd of told you that before she passed." He had walked inside his trailer. When he had come back with a can of Vienna sausages, Ben had stood up.

"You going?"

"Yeah. I got to get down to the station."

"That's good. Go put some fires out. Rescue you some kitty cats."

"That's what they pay me the big bucks for."

"Well, thank you for coming by to see your tired old daddy. You're a good boy. Your mama should've told you that before she passed."

"See you, Dad."

"You tell me how your trip goes," his father had yelled after Ben was in his truck. "You tell me how ol' Ocean Drive is doing these days."

On the corner of Ocean Boulevard and the Sea Mountain Highway, among the teenagers outside the arcade and the traffic flowing in for the weekend, Ben recalled how worried he'd been when Debra and Ginny were two hours late.

"I just walked down to here," he said to them. "Looking for y'all."

"What good did you think walking down here would do?" Ginny asked.

Ben shrugged. "Better than waiting."

"I'm sorry you were worried about us, baby," Debra said.

Ben shrugged again. "It's all right. Wasn't your fault."

"I know," Debra said, "but still." She put her arm behind his back, and brushed her fingers against his neck. "I should've tried to call again."

Ginny chewed her fingernails. "Traffic was an absolute bitch on that highway."

"It's fine," Ben said, driving landward, toward the bypass. On his waiting walk Ben had recalled all the collisions he'd responded to, and the length of Highways 9 and 501, the roads he'd told Ginny to take. He had recalled the strange turns the highways made in the mill-and-merchant, Main Street towns. He had recalled the fields as endless, and he had remembered the swamps as stalking.

"Was Lucas really upset?" Debra asked.

"Yeah. He'd been crying. I felt real bad about it."

"Oh, he'll be all right."

"I know, but still. I bet that did scare him, him waking up in a strange place and both of us not there."

"So you were sitting out on the curb," Ginny said, "because you thought we wouldn't find the condo?"

"I was afraid y'all might miss it in the dark."

"Well what if you'd missed us while you were taking your walk?"

"I was looking out for your car."

"In the dark?"

"I'd have seen you."

Debra patted Ben's thigh. "That sure was a long drive," she said.

On the other side of Business 17, out among the golf courses, out of any kind of Myrtle his father would recognize, Ben merged into the traffic on the bypass, going south.

"Now where is this place?" he asked.

"I'll tell you," Ginny said.

"Hope Lucas doesn't wake up," Ben said.

"He was out pretty solid," Debra said. She'd carried him inside when she and Ginny had finally arrived. She gave him milk and lay down beside him, stroking his hair until the cup fell from his hand.

He was out pretty solid when I went to wait for y'all, Ben thought. "He wouldn't have been so bad," he said, "if your mother'd left him alone."

"What do you mean, 'left him alone,'" Debra asked.

Ben downshifted for a red light. "After I got back she just kept going on about how scared he'd been, how he'd been crying. It just embarrassed him."

"She didn't mean nothing," Debra said.

"I didn't say she did, hon."

The light turned green and Ben climbed through the gears. "What's the name of this place again?"

"Banana Joe's," Ginny answered.

"And it's at Barefoot Landing?"

"Yes."

"And where's Barefoot Landing?"

"Right in front of you on the right."

With a sigh Ben slowed and waited for a suitable gap in the traffic closing in on him from behind. Seeing his chance, he stepped on the gas, gained speed across two lanes and entered the parking lot.

On the patio, overlooking the pond with a fountain rising from its heart, outside the front door of the bar he managed, Timmy Reed hugged each of the women.

"Goddamn, it's been a long time," he shouted, and once his arms were around he squeezed each of them tight. "Y'all have any trouble finding me?"

"Not a bit," Debra said.

"Sweet," Timmy said. "Sweet. Y'all eaten?"

"Yeah," Debra apologized. "We were running so late we got something on the road."

"I haven't had anything yet," Ben said.

"You haven't?" Timmy said, and extended his hand. "Oh, cool, man, hey, I'm Timmy Reed."

"Damn, baby, I'm sorry," Debra said. "Timmy, this is my husband Ben."

"Yeah, married now," Timmy said to Debra while he shook Ben's hand. "I don't know if I can think of you as anything but Debbie Hartselle, though, girl. Y'all come on in and I'll hook you up with a menu, my man."

On the barstool in the corner Ben recalled all he knew of Debra before they started dating, and all he found out later, while he busied himself with eating the roast beef sandwich in his hand. He had wanted to know everything; he wished there had been nothing to know. He wasn't sure why he cared, but he knew how the guys talked, sitting around the station house, and he knew he never wanted some other guy to know something about his wife that he didn't. He asked her to tell. None of what she told him changed her from the woman he loved, or took away the virtues he'd come to trust in her. Most of it he blamed on the failures of her parents, her mother unrelenting and her father cold and unhappy. Debra named for him all her boyfriends. She confessed to the nights with friends who she thought would stay friends. She confessed to the nights with someone she'd just met. But she refused to give him a number. She promised she'd warn him if he ever had to meet one.

"How's that sandwich, man," Timmy asked him. "Want another beer?"

Mouth full, Ben shook his head no.

"Didn't Chris Peele come live down here?" Debra asked.

"Oh, shit yeah. We came down here together," Timmy said. He leaned on the barstool next to Ginny's.

"Is he still down here?"

"Shoot. Yeah. You wouldn't believe what he's doing now."

"What?"

"Now, you remember that Chris is a crazy son of a bitch, right?"

"Yeah –"

"Motherfucker is a bullrider over at the OK Roundup."

Ginny slapped him on the shoulder.

"Bullshit."

"Nope. Straight up."

"Holy shit."

"Yep."

Ben swallowed. "What's the OK Roundup?"

"It's this Old West theme restaurant down on King's Highway. You get to watch a rodeo and a fake gunfight and shit while you eat your big-ass steak."

"How did Chris get to be a bullrider?" Debra asked

"He got a job down there washing dishes. One day they needed a bullrider 'cause the old one had broke his neck or took a horn up the ass or something. Chris stepped up and was like, 'Uh, yeah, I know how to ride a bull.' Dude, what the hell."

"Oh, man," Debra said, "that's the shit."

On his last bite of sandwich Ben recalled all the failings Debra had listed in all her early boys: reckless and slackass, convinced of what they deserved, fine with doing boys' work for the rest of their lives. They sounded a lot like his father.

"You like that sandwich?" Timmy asked him.

Ben nodded. "Real good."

"Glad you liked it, man. On me. It's on me. Can I get you another beer?"

Ben looked at what was left of his first. "No, I'm all right."

"Come on. It's on me."

It's on the owner, Ben thought. "No, I'm good, thanks."

"Come on, man, you're making me nervous here."

Ben waited for the women to stop laughing. "No, I'm fine. Don't be nervous."

"All right. Fair enough," Timmy said. "I got to check on a few things, y'all. I'll be right back." He turned to smile at Ginny as he left.

"So," Debra said, leaning away from Ben, "will you need a ride home tonight or not?"

"Yes," Ginny said quickly. "God yes. Tomorrow night. I've waited this long."

"Ooh," Debra teased, "you're a patient woman."

"I guess I," Ginny teased back, "just don't know what I'm missing."

Debra smiled, and sat upright on her stool.

"Where you living now?" Timmy asked Debra as he sat back down.

"We got a house out near Mint Hill."

"Kicking it over on the east side, huh?"

"Yeah, done left the west side behind."

"That ain't hard to do. Once you cross that interstate it's like you're in a different world."

"That's why I don't cross the interstate anymore," Debra said.

"So I guess you don't see much of our old buds anymore?"

"Not many of them that I want to see."

"You like it out in Mint Hill?"

Debra nodded.

"I grew up out there," Ben said.

"Oh. Stole her away from us, huh?" Timmy smiled. Timmy hadn't stopped smiling.

Ben smiled. "Guess so." He considered what would be the last swallow of his beer. "Y'all ready to head on when I finish this?"

Debra's mother asked after Timmy the next day. She asked when Ben and Debra left their bedroom, she asked again while they sat out on the beach. She asked Debra to describe the bar Timmy managed when they sat down in Hardee's to eat lunch.

In the afternoon they drove to the outlet mall. Ben went with them into every store, checking out kitchenware, women's clothes, housewares, children's clothes. When asked he tried his best to have an opinion. Leaving one store, holding the door, he looked across the parking lot and the highway and saw one of the brand-new NASCAR

Cafés. The white walls rose from a small, grassy rise, and were topped by rippling flags. Ben had read that every one of those places was full of tokens from all the great drivers: one of Earnhardt's cars, one of Petty's helmets, one of Cale's jumpsuits, all battered and burned by the headlong force of their job. Beside the café was a go-kart track.

"Honey," Ben said, "how 'bout I take Lucas, and me and him go over there while y'all shop?" He pointed to the NASCAR Café.

"Oh, baby, we're almost done here. I promise. And then we'll head back to the condo and get back out on the beach for a little while."

"All right," Ben said.

But they spent an hour on the bypass, traffic was so thick, and Lucas cried when told they wouldn't have time for the beach. Timmy Reed was coming by to take them out to dinner, and they had to get ready. Ben changed his shirt, and asked Debra if she'd mind if he took a short walk.

The beach was clearing as the evening drew near. Ben walked on the hard-packed sand near the tide. He stepped aside for a pair of surfcasters, and passed a group of boys playing football. Four on four, they played loudly, without their heads in the game. They shoved and showed off for the girls laid out on blankets on the loose, hot sand beneath the dunes. Ben could see through the boys' game that the girls were either watching or pretending not to watch. One rolled over, twitching her ass in the air as she smoothed out her blanket, untying her top as she lay down on her chest.

In between downs the boys eyed him, holding their new muscles tight and their hands ready at their sides. Ben watched them back, evenly, unafraid of any wildness these boys might threaten him with.

He soon reached the end of the beach, where storms had carved an inlet through the sand, and where the tides were still carving more. In the ruins of blacktop Ben stood looking at the other side. Across the inlet was a marshy beach topped with sea oats. Swim across, he suddenly thought, it might be fun. The tide was out, and the inlet was shallow; he could wade most of the way.

But it'd be silly to show up back at the condo wet. The tide could come back in and strand him. He would have no explanation for Debra and she was looking forward to dinner. He had run without hesitation into rooms more full of fire than air. He had done so with a purpose. He had no purpose on the other side, no point in wading into unknown water, other than the slim chance of some enjoyment.

His father had once told him about cruising past the Pavilion with one of his greasy buddies when they saw a girl walk by in a leather bikini. His father jumped out of the car while it was still moving and ran into the girl's path. He was about to say hello when the girl looked at him and said, "Why, you're Calvin Cooper, ain't you?" Turns out his father was famous all up and down the Strip, and up and down the mill hills that kept the Strip supplied. Being a crazy son-of-a-bitch was enough to make you a hero.

You're goddamn right I never came down here, you prick, Ben thought. I was doing the job you should have done, and Mom always told me how grateful she was.

On the beach after dinner Ben and Debra sat holding hands. They sat on a porch overlooking the sea. The tide was back in, licking at the pilings at the base of the dunes. Debra explained the history between Ginny and Timmy Reed.

"They dated in high school," she said. "Yeah, for like a couple of years. But this is the first time they've gotten together like this. Ginny was a virgin back then."

Ben nodded, staring at the sand, unable to think of anything he wanted to hear less, but feeling like something depended on him listening.

"She was like a big-time prep back then. Pretty little popular girl. So yeah, they've been waiting for tonight for a long time. That's why Ginny's been a little more bitchy than usual."

"That why they broke up?" Ben asked. "'Cause she wouldn't?"

"Sort of," Debra said. "You know, Ginny and I weren't really friends in high school. Like I said, she was all preppy and popular. We mainly just knew each other through Timmy."

"You and him were friends?"

"Yeah. We were real good friends."

The waves collapsed on the shore and skimmed up the sand. Invisible in the dark, they made a sizzling sound. The lights of the Pavilion and the Strip were a smudge on the southern horizon; the lights of Ocean Drive blinked inconstantly. On the ocean at night, Ben recalled being told, a lit match can be seen for many miles. He was short of breath. He wanted to stand and shout: You promised you'd never make a fool of me.

"I need to take a walk," he said.

"Right now?" Debra clutched at his fingers as he stood up. "Baby, the tide's in."

"I know." Ben looked her in the eye, terrified, realizing that he might start to cry. He knew how desperately they were tied to each other. She knew he had figured it out.

"Honey," she said.

"I'll be back, soon. I won't be gone long." He climbed down off the porch, sinking into the water and wet sand. He could not understand how hurt he was. He was hurt for the promise his wife had broken. He was hurt that she once wanted release with a faithless and frustrated boy. He was hurt by the careless play of so many surrounding him, and by the safety and protection that allowed it. Slogging and dutiful, still trying not to cry, he walked slowly in the dark toward the end of the beach.

The Death of John Gardiner

That Christmas Eve was wet, and just cold enough that ice was a threat.

"Your mother fixed a good dinner," John Gardiner said as Will Adams drove.

"She did. She usually does."

Gardiner was silent except for his watery breathing. "I hope she knows how much her mother and I appreciate her," he eventually said. He needed half a minute to say this, and he coughed when he was finished. When he finished coughing he took a puff on the cigar that he had snuck past his wife.

"I think she does," Will said. "I know she's happy to do it. She's happy to be able to do it."

John Gardiner nodded. He stared out the window, watching the thin woods and hemmed fields pass by, watching how the brown high grass of the Catawba valley had shrunk in this weather. Will wanted to think he was remembering the abundant woods and fields that filled the valley when he was a boy, and remembering how much he missed that abundance. Will wanted to think he was reflecting on how the woods and fields had receded since then, and reflecting on the part he had played in that. As a boy John Gardiner had helped his father bring trees down, haul them with hooks and chains out of the woods, and saw them into lumber. In his retirement he invested in development, in housing tracts, condos, and shopping centers. From Hickory to the west side of Charlotte he had helped remake the valley. Will wanted to think he was remembering deer hunts and turkey shoots.

Will parked the van under the clinic's carport. He took his grandfather's wheelchair from the back and unfolded it next to the passenger door.

"You want to finish that cigar before we go in?" Will asked. Gardiner shook his head. He set it gently on the edge of the ashtray. Will had been told not to help him out of the car or into the wheelchair. He held the chair still while his grandfather raised himself from his seat and lowered himself into the wheelchair, and before Will started to push John Gardiner was shuffling the chair forward with his slippered feet.

Gardiner looked back at the van. "Hand me that there," he told Will, flipping a shaky hand at the dashboard. Will fetched the cigar. Gardiner shuffled toward the canister outside the front door, with Will pushing gently behind. He did not put out the cigar. He tapped off the ash and shuffled on toward the door.

"Pappy," Will said, eyeing the No Smoking and Oxygen In Use signs, "they're not going to let you in there with that."

Gardiner blew a plume of smoke into the air. "I'll hide it," he said, with what sounded to Will almost like a snarl.

On gurneys and in wheelchairs those who lived in the clinic clustered just inside the sliding doors. They watched Gardiner and his grandson with no expression that Will could read, but then he could not look them in the eyes for very long. Nurses and candy stripers bustled around and behind the central desk. Gardiner shuffled forward.

'Damned if I'm going to be the dork here,' Will thought. The doors slid open. John Gardiner and his grandson, a slight column of smoke trailing behind them, passed through the lobby without notice or comment. Down the length of the hall Will couldn't wait to tell his mother about this.

They were met at the room by the candy striper who had signed Gardiner out that morning. She fluttered in, walking quickly on short legs, and took the handles of the wheelchair from Will.

"I bet y'all ain't changed him since he's been at the house, have you?" she said.

"No, I'm pretty sure we haven't."

"Well I'll go 'head and change him while you sign him back in. Come on, Mr. Gardiner, let's wheel you right into the bathroom and—good Lord, Mr. Gardiner, you can't have that in here."

John Gardiner didn't argue with her, and he certainly didn't plead. He just said, "I'll finish it in the bathroom," and shuffled through the bathroom door.

"No, no, Mr. Gardiner, I can't let you smoke that thing in here, we'd both get in trouble." She took the cigar from his fingers and dropped it into the toilet bowl. He at least managed to arch an eyebrow.

"You go on and sign him in now," she said to Will. "I don't know what you were thinking, anyway, letting him in here with that."

Will was still thinking that he couldn't wait to tell his family about this. He was thinking how much he'd like a cigar himself. Will Adams was thinking, in some channel of his mind, of mythology, of all he'd ever heard from or about John Gardiner, of how his grandfather was now left with only the force assembled in the stories about him, of how the knowledge of those stories made this wheelchair-bound husk of John Gardiner more powerful than either this woman or Will himself. He was thinking of which story he could or should tell her to give her an idea, to bring a part of the power of personal legend to bear:

When he was in California (where he'd hitchhiked, by the way, to work on airplanes, the day after high school ended, because the Washington Senators hadn't signed him, as he thought they might), Joe Louis made a morale-boosting tour of the factory floor. Being a teenage backwoods hick from North Carolina, my grandfather refused to shake the champ's hand. Years later he was on one of his many trips to Las Vegas (where often he won enough at cards to pay for the entire trip) and Joe Louis, in his sad decline, was working as a casino greeter. John Gardiner walked up to him, shook his hand, and told him about his ignorance two decades and two wars before. Joe Louis smiled at him and said, "That's really bothered you all these years, hasn't it?" My grandfather said, "Yes—yes it has." Joe Louis leaned in close to him and said, "Hasn't bothered me a bit."

In the war he was a turret gunner on an A-20 attack bomber, sitting alone in a plexiglass bubble on top of the plane, he and his .88 millimeter the only thing between him and his crew and the Zeroes. On one mission they had to blow up a dam in the Phillippines, a dam built deep in a gorge between two peaks. The Japanese had built anti-aircraft batteries into the cliffs, and as the bomber dove the guns followed, shooting down on them from above. John Gardiner fired back, and since he was there to tell and I was there to listen, he must have aimed well. He and I sat in his den, with a baseball game on TV, back when he lived with my grandmother in their own house. I had to beg him to tell me this story. He told it, and then he said, "I didn't know until then what those big .88 slugs did to a human body," and then I watched my grandfather cry.

"I was thinking that the man wanted his cigar," Will told the candy striper. He left the room and walked to the nurses' station.

Stories had been told, existed and were out there, about John Gardiner's toughness, his shrewdness, his audacity. Images were still around, like the photograph of him on the deck of a cruise ship, looking lean and expert with a shotgun in his hands, shooting skeet off the stern. Finally prosperous, his back to the camera, in the photo he represented to Will an entire population on the move, off of the farms and out of the woods and into the commerce of postwar America, wily and rugged and tempered, claiming their part of the nation that their wildness and violence had saved and rebuilt. No war has been won without backcountry boys who are comfortable with blood, who can shoot like they can point.

Will had a favorite story. His grandfather liked to tell of his time in London, when the Air Force called up the reserves during the Korean War. Gardiner and his squadron got no further east than England.

"This was in 1951," Gardiner liked to say, "and I was in a club having a drink with this old Brit who liked to talk politics with me. I told him that by 1955 Dwight Eisenhower would be president of the United States and Winston Churchill would be prime minister again. And do you know that that old man laughed at me?" Then John Gardiner liked to laugh himself.

Will was almost thirty, and had lived in London himself, before he asked his grandfather: "What were you doing in one of those clubs in the first place? I mean, they don't hand out memberships to those on the tube. I lived in London for half a year and don't even know where one is."

Gardiner lived in his own house then, the house that he had retired to on a Lincoln County cove of Lake Norman. The water was sparkling; the wind was blowing across the face of the water. Will had come up from Charlotte to spend a few hours. Gardiner took several deep breaths, collecting his thoughts.

"I had a friend who was a member. He arranged for me to have a temporary membership for the duration I was stationed over there."

"How'd you meet him? And how'd you become such good friends that he'd do that?"

"Several of us were in a hotel bar one night. I was the only one that was married. And there was this Australian who kept getting louder and louder the more he drank. Some of the guys I was with started mouthing off to him, and he started mouthing back, and—these were just boys, now. I stepped in and he and I jawed for a while, and I was fixing to knock his teeth down his throat. But this waitress that knew us both got between us and told us we didn't want to do that, and she was right. Turned out he had been a commando during the war, part of a team that went into the jungles on these islands in the south Pacific to rescue downed fliers. So no doubt he had saved some of my buddies at one time or another. So I bought him a round and he bought me a round.

"Well, before I left I thanked that waitress and she and I got to talking a little bit, and she said she'd always been fond of me since we started coming in there because I looked just like her husband that had been killed in the war. She lived with her brother in this little flat, and she said I ought to come have dinner with them sometime.

"I did. And I tell you, Billy—when I saw the picture of her husband—the resemblance was uncanny." Gardiner shook his head. "They still had the wartime rationing going on then. Her brother and I hit it off. He was a writer for the *Times of London*. He was the one who got me into his club."

The wind moved across the water. Will had more questions than before, but John Gardiner seemed tired.

Will drove home and called his mother to see if she had ever heard this story. "He was real good friends with a brother and sister over there," she said. "They stayed in touch for years, until they died. They went to see them every time they went to England. He does that—usually he can't be bothered to hold a two-minute conversation, but every now and then he'll get to talking to somebody and they're devoted to him for life. I never heard the rest of that, though. You never know with him."

Will sat that night staring at a blank sheet of paper, conjuring up a London that his grandfather might have known. Accurate scholarship could re-create what had been bombed out, what had been rebuilt, what had been replaced, what was still rubble in 1951. He could get his hands on a Pevsner's guide and figure out what stood while his grandfather was stationed there. From his own life in London he could imagine the rudiments of landscape: the white Regency line along St. James; the slow, straight rise from Westminster to Trafalgar Square; the rush and confusion of the Imperial capital. John Gardiner hadn't said where the flat was, or which hotel the sister worked in, and Will wondered if he remembered. Will wondered if he'd made that part up. John Gardiner could bluff without blinking. Will had once asked him what a particular movie was about, and Gardiner had rattled off the voiceover prologue as if the words were his own eloquent insights. Will knew only two other people who could not just remember but steal like that, and Will himself was one of them.

If John Gardiner knew by then what Will did, that his personal force was reduced to his bank account and his history, then why would he not do all he could to make his history as strong as possible? If that history was not to be trusted, what was left of his power? If little was left of his power, what was left of the only inheritance that mattered to Will?

When Will returned from signing him in, John Gardiner was in bed, looking exhausted.

"Can I get you anything?" Will asked. He had other questions.

Gardiner shook his head and tried to clear his throat. He raised one knee so that his pants leg draped over his wasted, bony thigh. Will noticed that his grandfather's wrists and ankles were the size of a child's.

The candy striper brought a large plastic cup that she had filled with water. "Now you just press that button if you need anything," she called out as she left. Will watched her leave. He knew he would not get to ask his questions.

"I better head on back," he said. "You best get some rest."

Gardiner nodded. His words came in long intervals. "You take care. You take care of those kids." He nodded again. "You're doing good, Billy."

Will put his hand on his grandfather's shoulder, and squeezed with restraint. "I'll see you again soon." Gardiner looked up at him. Will slowly bent over and kissed his grandfather's cheek.

Through the open doors along the hall Will could see pictures of men in uniforms, young conquerors looking mighty and glad to be alive. Those same men lay in beds and watched old movies on TV, surrounded by children and grandchildren who sat tentatively bedside, sharing time. Through the open doors Will could hear the children gossip—Mr. Henderson from the church, he fell and broke his hip; no one likes the new preacher; Mizzus Abernathy at the store, she finally retired. Will saw a son-in-law change the channels, saw a granddaughter hold Christmas cards up and heard her read them aloud, saw a daughter hold her mother upright while she coughed up phlegm and blood, while her body shuddered and shook. Will saw women growing old, holding the hands of their mothers and fathers, exchanging what they could while they still had time.

Back at the duplex, Will thought as he drove from the clinic, my children will be spread out on the floor with their uncle, loudly playing a new game. His wife, my wife, our sister, our mother and father, our grandmother, will be seated around them, smiling and sleepy. Christmas music will be playing or a ballgame will be on TV. The room will be warm.

As he drove the rain began to fall again. Will thought of a brief prayer, asking that the wet roads from here to home not freeze. After the prayer he thought of a briefer thanksgiving, that ice was the most imminent danger he had to fear. He thought of a longer thanksgiving for all he was allowed, and for all that the generations had done that he would be allowed to avoid.

Before they drove home they would drive down the valley, following his brother Luke to another Catawba mill town, where his brother would preach the Christmas sermon to the town's stagnant middle class. Luke had talked over his sermon with Will, had tested out his themes and parables, that morning before they ate dinner. Luke wanted to preach on Hauerwas's critique of Neibuhr, on Augustine's cities and just wars, on the problems of the Constantinian shift and the fallacy of the so-called Christian nation. He and Will parried, honing thoughts, providing examples and counter-examples from philosophy and from Scripture, quoting, dragging in Kierkegaard and Chesterton, showing off their luxurious educations. In the midst of this Will looked up to see his grandfather in his big chair across the room, listening to them, looking amused and happy, looking grateful and justified.

Drowning and infected, John Gardiner stopped breathing that March. In the funeral home the next day, his widow and his daughter asked Will Adams to write the obituary. The week before, Will had begun a new poem, trying to build some kind of frame or explanation, and he had that typescript in the breast pocket of his jacket. He took out that paper and his pen and went with his mother into the hallway. She shook her hands relentlessly. She gave him bare facts: positions, titles, years, memberships; and Will realized that she gave them to him in the unasked hope that he could turn them, concisely, into something like what they had known of John Gardiner.

The Playground of the Fearless

"Where are you guys from?" the man in the leather blazer asked.

"Charlotte," Will Adams replied.

"Where's that?" the man asked.

Will turned a detached smile, the only proper response, to this small blow to his city's aspirations. "North Carolina," he said.

"Oh, well," the man said, "you probably won't want to publish my book then, but I'm going to tell you about it anyway 'cause you need to know this stuff." From a bag made of the same leather as his coat, the man pulled a color-copied flier and handed it to Will.

"It's called *The Playground of the Fearless*," the man said. "It's an alternative history of New York City. It's got all the stuff in there, the real stuff, the stuff that the eggheads either won't tell you 'cause it isn't all respectable, or can't tell you 'cause they might get their dainty little fingers dirty finding out about it."

"That so?" Will said, turning to look behind him. Two of his colleagues from the university press were busy dismantling their trade show booth. "Y'all sure you don't need my help?" Will asked.

"Oh, no," Virginia Roe said with a smile. "Not at all."

"Anyway," the man in the leather coat said, "like I was saying. It's called *The Playground of the Fearless*, 'cause that's what New York is, see? I start at the very beginning. You know who was the first to settle Manhattan, right?"

"Native Americans?"

"No, the Dutch. Peter Minute bought it from the Indians for 23 clam shells. That's where the phrase 'New York Minute' comes from.

"Now, see, a lot of your egghead historians will tell you how Peter Minute ripped off those Indians, what with paying 23 clam shells for the whole island of Manhattan. But see, this is how come my book is so important, because what I tell you is that those Indians, they were the ones who ripped off Peter Minute. They wanted to get rid of the place."

"They did?"

"You better believe they did. You know why they did?" His leather coat loudly crinkled as the man leaned in. "'Cause they knew what was lurking on this island."

The man talked on, of conspiracies, taboo knowledge, secret signs. The earliest settlers didn't find an earthly paradise here, he said, or a "tabula rosa" (a rose slate? Will wanted to ask but didn't) to build on. They found temptations waiting in the woods, demons in the trees, corrupting them at every turn. "Read your Washington Irving. Read Poe. They knew what was out there."

The man talked on. He said that New York became a cauldron, not a melting pot, a devil's Colisseum where each new immigrant tribe had to fight for its place, and its American chance to make money and take power. "You see? Demons waiting for them."

"So how does that make New York any different from the rest of America?" Will asked.

The man's face broke apart in glee, and he clapped his hands loudly, once. "Exactly!" he shouted. People turned to look.

The man in the leather coat adjusted the weight of his bag and started to walk away from Will. He pointed at the flier he'd left in Will's hand, and at Will's face. "You remember this," he said. "It's important."

Will nodded and waved goodbye. Reading the flier, he saw an e-mail address but no name. The more he read the more he recognized every idea the man spouted as some other writer's; the man in the leather blazer had just collected and forced them together. Another recollection, a recent one, jarred him: on Columbus Avenue, getting into a taxi, an ad bolted to its roof. An art exhibit opening soon—WELCOME TO THE PLAYGROUND OF THE FEARLESS. The man had stolen even his title.

"I warned you about the show's last day," Virginia said to Will. "Can you reach those light bulbs?"

The would-be authors with their one-day passes came out on Sunday, carrying bags that carried copies of their manuscripts with fliers they had paid to have produced. They sniffed out a small, unintimidating press, presumably desperate; they cornered its representative, talked at length and without doubt. Their writings on conspiracy, on hidden powers and designs, were the finest in the field, would be remembered for centuries, had a right to be published. Their life story was so much different from anyone else's, they had a story that deserved wide readership, their story had a right to be published. Will saw a woman pushing a wheelchair that held an enormous man, who demanded she stop at every publisher's booth. With great diginity he would take from a canvas bag a flier, an advertisement for his self-published book, and bestow it upon the publisher now before him. He would not speak, except to order the woman on to the next booth when he was done. In his wake rolled a thousand eyes; a hundred ironic brows were raised.

Will was in New York to help launch the press's new Metrolina Voices™ poetry series. Will was the poetry editor; his work had appeared in respectable venues. He had some credibility. He was supposed to explain, to the sales reps and the media and the booksellers, why the poets in the series were significant, accomplished, worth attention and placement. "Nobody expects to sell any poetry," Walker Donovan had explained in a cab when they first arrived. Donovan was the press's director. "It's a prestige thing. We're a brand new press. This is a good way to get our name out there."

"You can answer their questions," Virginia had added, "give them a handle on the books." Virginia was in charge of marketing. "Give them something to compare it to. A sound bite they can take to the booksellers."

In suites at the Yale Club and the Mayflower Hotel, in meeting rooms at *Publishers' Weekly* and the *New York Times*, Will had done what he needed to do. He was surprised and disturbed—he was really, really good at it. Will had no use for the aloof purity invoked by some writers in the name of their craft, because every writer he had ever known expected to be published and then to be read. For that to happen in this overflowing market, things had to be done, even or especially by publishers sponsored by a state university. He had long before ceased to believe that any kind of writing was sacred: important, vital, crucial, but never sacred, never entitled, never untouchable. Still, he hadn't expected to take to marketing this well. His words were concise, and contained just enough academic jargon to be heard. His meanings were clear, and even reasonable. He kept corresponding examples at his beck and call, and they always proved useful and enlightening.

At the Book Expo, Will had had few chances to repeat himself. The attendees hustled through the lobby of the convention center, warily eyeing the vaults of glass above them, waving their laminated passes preemptively at the cops and the ushers. Most of the people weaving by the press's small booth on the trade show floor were on the lookout for freebies and celebrities. Most who stopped were interested in non-fiction. If they asked about poets they asked which famous poets they wrote like, or they talked about their own poems. They took advance galleys and free postcards. Rumors and hype swept the show floor along variable circuits. Report of sightings—LL Cool J downstairs, Dr. Ruth roaming the aisles—predominated, but shared the floor with the kindling of mass opinion. No more than six of the right people had to ask, "Have you read the new ____?" within a one hour period before all attendees, by the end of the day or the start of the next, had to have ____'s galley. They took ____'s galley back to their stores and their features editors.

"The thing is," Donovan explained to Will, "that nine times out of ten, ____ is really pretty good. Maybe not a classic, but maybe so, and awfully good, at the very least." Careers were made. The seeds were sown for two-week notices; schools lost teachers, bookstores lost clerks, newspapers lost beat reporters. Publishers lost editors.

As the Book Expo slouched towards its end, Will helped Walker and Virginia dismantle the display, pack the leftover books in boxes, affix the shipping labels. Clutching their satchels and suitcases, stuffed with free books, they made their way out of the exhibit hall and into the open air. Walker and Virginia were going home; they had arranged already for a shuttle to the airport, and as they climbed in they said goodbye to Will. Will was staying for one more night; he was staying to see some old friends. He pushed his sleeve up his forearm to look at his watch. He had to move. The line for taxis stretched the length of the convention center, twice, but Will had secret knowledge. He walked east, uphill from the river, among the bristle of spires grown uptown and downtown around him. The towers of Manhattan had reflected nothing but brilliance when Will arrived four days ago, when the plane ran down the Hudson toward the morning sun. From his window seat he could peer down the long straight furrows of the crosstown streets. He could see the piers, prickly as quills, coming quickly one after another to the tip of the island.

Then the plane had banked and changed course, toward the runway at Newark, and through his window Will looked down on a ziggurat of steel containers, multihued and stamped with tracking numbers and logos. Only the scale was unfamiliar; Will had spent more time than he wanted to sweating in dusty truckyards, working a lowly and indispensable job, delivering truck parts to shipping lines lodged between cris-crossing interstates. He had never seen, though, such an assembly of cargo. The dusky metal boxes beneath him were stacked several stories high, uneasily high, and he teased himself imagining where they all could have come from and where they all would go. He saw the monstrous cranes, and he could see containers being hitched onto trains and trucks and sent off into the continent. Seeing the cargo yard had reminded him of honest work, of how he, and the sunlit towers, had come to be.

In the taxi that took him from the airport Will had looked for the New York skyline he'd seen from the air. Instead he saw New Jersey road work, razor wire, row houses on sloping streets, a prison and its prisoners behind the triple fence, a multiplex, a shopping mall, and, just before his cab entered the Lincoln Tunnel, a lonely roadside stand of golden reeds swaying in the wind. He stared at the unexpected plant life, the same kind of reeds he'd seen in tidal marshes along the Southern coasts, the same kind of tidal marsh biding its time beneath the expressway. The traffic trying to enter the tunnel was more than the tunnel's mouth could take, so as the cab crept forward by inches Will could watch the reeds wave for what seemed like a long time. He watched these reeds as marsh reeds had been watched from dugout canoes and daub-and-wattle huts, by fishermen casting nets by hand and by hunters stalking beside the river; by the first plump sailed, Protestant ships plowing into the harbor, and by sailboats and steamboats plying the river for trade. The taxi and the overwhelming traffic had circled down the bluffs toward the tunnel, while Will imagined commerce beating ceaselessly on the eastern shore, hammering up the rivers until the vast, flush interior was beaten down, taken from its first owners and made available. He had imagined the sudden, violent deaths demanded by tribal wars, trade wars, floods, fires and factory deaths. He had tried to feel the courage and cruelty demanded by the building. Lately he had been thinking a lot about all that. He had shuddered when the cab came up inside New York. As soon as he had reached his Midtown hotel he called his wife Mary, to let her know he'd arrived safely.

Leaving the end of the trade show, he wanted to get back to his hotel in time to call Mary again. He walked quickly. On Eighth Avenue he hailed a cab, gave the driver his hotel's address, and told him to hurry. Through the crowds of the Sunday afternoon the driver made good time, driving creatively. A march had been held that day, to celebrate the sovereignty of Israel, and protesters for a free Palestine had lined the course of the march. Today had also been Cuban-American Day, and protesters had been out calling for an end to economic sanctions. A group of bicyclists had pedaled through Midtown, to promote bicycling as pollutionless transport. The stragglers and drift of all this mingled with the tourists and the usual movement of Manhattan, and stood in the way of oncoming traffic. Against all this the cab driver—his name was Goran, and he was from Croatia, where what was left of his family still lived—made good time, and stopped in front of Will's hotel before the market next door brought its flowers in off the sidewalk. Will tipped Goran generously. In the market he pulled a rose from its bucket and paid for it. In his room he removed his tie and draped it over a chair. He sat on the bed and called his wife.

During his four days in New York, Will had wandered through Midtown, passed by other people, coming at him or coming from behind, moving too fast for him to watch closely; they stared straight ahead and their eyes mirrored dull static. He had walked by Rockefeller Center, the cathedral, the stores on Fifth Avenue. He'd walked through Grand Central Station, the Met and Central Park. He'd ridden the subway. He had walked through Hell's Kitchen one morning, but he didn't know it at the time, because the neighborhood was called something else now. Another morning, not long after midnight, Will had walked the circuit of Times Square, his eyes and feet moving fast and subtly in the artificial day. He had turned a detached smile, the only proper response, to the digitized faces above him, selling new albums, movies and shows, selling luxury products or food, selling one of the population's ideas of itself. The famous streetscape had turned into pixils. The fonts and graphics of the season were aggressively happy, suggesting a knowing innocence, a worldly naivete, a frail and skinny greed. The restaurants around the square were comforting, familiar from most of the better malls. Networks streamed from here into living rooms. Up Broadway Will had followed a flock of boys in baggy jeans and backwards ball caps, loud and eager to inflict their energy. Part of him had hoped they'd start something. He had walked up the Bowery, past CBGB's. He had seen or done everything in New York he wanted to see or do, except for one thing. He would do that soon. He told his wife he loved her and hung up the phone.

From his bag he took a newspaper and returned to the lobby. He sat in a chair that gave him a view of the sidewalk. Sean and Claire McManus arrived before he had read much of the paper.

They greeted each other happily: how have you been, how about y'all, how are your parents, how are Mary and the kids, are you ready to see them again? Glad to be in each other's company, they walked to the nearest subway station and waited on the platform for the number one train downtown. At Sean's asking, Will told them about this new job he had, about the books he'd already edited, about the Book Expo he was in town for. He told them money and time were actually tighter than they had been when he ran the parts warehouse, which did not make Mary happy, but she was happy knowing he enjoyed his new job more than his old. He told them he felt a vague, daily compromise. He told them he was a good editor who was quickly earning professional respect. He told them he had seen LL Cool J at the trade show.

"Ladies Love Cool James," Sean said.

"Apparently so," Will said.

"My mom was real glad to hear that you'd taken this job," Sean said. "She said she feels a whole lot better about the future knowing your brain's back in the game."

Will shrugged and his face turned red. "We make choices in our youth," he said. He was not quite thirty. When he was twenty-three he chose to leave what he thought was inauthentic—studying literature—for what was more authentic—toting the drums and clutches that would keep the truck fleet moving. He asked himself what made him think that way, what made him think that graduate school was any less the real world than a truckyard: proximity of dirt, emphasis on the mechanical body, chance of violent harm? Was it that none of the people he came from had ever spent as much time in school as he had, or that all the people he came from wanted him so badly to stay? When he took a job as poetry editor for a university press, he heard a lot of told-you-so's and about-time's. He didn't argue, but he knew the facts. He was stronger now. He was braver now, to the edge of cruelty. Without question his old job had made him better prepared for the real work of his life than school would have alone. "It seemed real romantic there for a while," he said.

They heard a clatter uptown, turned and saw the tunnel light up, saw the light intensify and heard the clatter come towards them. The brakes screamed against the rails, the doors slid open with a pneumatic hiss, and they boarded and found seats. Sean and Will told stories from college, crazy shit they'd seen, done or heard about. Will was glad to tell these stories again, when they seemed so lame next to Mary's. They told Claire about turning the Waffle House on Highway 52 into their personal, twenty-four-hour study hall, "because the library's no help when you don't start studying until midnight," Will explained, adding that from the library, you couldn't watch the sunrise climb Pilot Mountain. They remembered the time they tried to sneak Kate Sawyer, barefoot, into the old Sampler's on University Parkway, and how she started giggling uncontrollably when she saw the back table full of uniformed cops. They remembered senior year when they challenged the pledges to a paintball war out in Surry County, and how after several hours and more than a few beers they were throwing rocks and tackling each other in the brush. They remembered getting into the fine arts building after hours and playing all-night hide-and-seek in its miles of corridors, concert rooms, studios, stages. They remembered sneaking into the campus's underground tunnels. They relived the mud slides on the Quad after Wake beat Duke. They told Claire about the dance they took Kate and Annie Rayburn to, "not as couples but as a quartet, you know?" and how Kate and Annie started giving them shit for not buying them flowers. "So we went to a grocery store," Will said to Claire, "and made them wait in the parking lot while we went in and bought them what had to be the ugliest flowers in the history of horticulture." They told stories of how the world seemed to open before them then, stories that involved passports and backpacks, savings from summer jobs. They talked about that long, rainy night drive to the beach, when they passed deserted crossroads and talked about stopping just to see who'd show up.

Claire leaned over to whisper something to Sean. Will stared straight ahead, but there was no light outside the car and the windows had turned into mirrors. He was embarrassed to look at himself, and embarrassed to look at the strangers around him—an old woman clutching a worn purse and a young couple who looked like they were ending a day in the city. He saw the reflection of Sean and Claire talking privately and tried not to listen to their whispers. He read the map of the subway posted on the wall, and read the ads that flanked it: evening classes to get an MBA, hair removal techniques, allergy medicine.

"You travel a path on paper," Sean said out loud, to the subway car in general, "and discover you're in a city you only thought about before." Sean was leaning to the side, into Claire, looking straight above them, reading the poem printed on the placard.

Will looked at the reflections in the window. The old woman had not moved or shifted her gaze. The young couple stared at Sean for a moment, maybe less; the young man smiled maliciously and said something softly in Spanish to the girl, who laughed.

"You are still writing, aren't you?" Sean asked Will.

"When I can. I haven't sent anything off in a while."

"Be sure to send me some stuff. You never know when I might need to get out of a ticket." Sean grinned at his wife. "One of Will's poems got me out of a ticket once. I was living in Providence and Will came to see me. He gave me some new poems he'd written. I was reading one of them while I drove in to work at Delvecchio's, and a state trooper pulled me over.

"He asked what I was reading while I drove on his highway. I said, 'Oh, it's a poem a friend of mine wrote.'

"He said, 'What's it about?'

"I said, 'You know, the stuff poems are usually about—he's in love with this girl and it's not going well.'

"He said, 'Give it here.'

"So he stood there beside my car on the side of the road and read Will's poem, and when he was done, he handed it back to me, kind of nodded, and said, 'That's pretty good. Next time read it at home.' And he got back in his cruiser and drove away."

Claire looked at Will. "Bullshit."

Will shrugged. "I wasn't there."

"Hand to God," Sean said. "It happened just like that."

He went on to tell, or prompted Will to tell, more stories from when they were younger, so that when they rose from the Chambers Street station they were laughing. While they rode the subway the sun had not set. The May dusk was a deeper blue in the chasms of the street. They walked downtown on West Broadway. Will felt cool shivers run from his stomach to the ends of his limbs.

He began to see mud caked and dried on the street, mud tracked with the treads of heavy tires. He looked down the sidewalk as far as he could see. Sean and Claire were holding hands. Twenty yards ahead a handful stood still, lined up along the cross street, and a cop leaned against a sawhorse.

In less than a year the events and idea of history had telescoped, pushing the recent past into the dark of distant memory. Will had felt time pass like this before. His first semester in college, his first months studying in London, the first few years of his marriage: whenever the plot of his life took a turn instead of a curve, the days passed quickly, and soon the commencement turned into a memory as far away and unclear as the memories of his childhood, too vast to be easily recalled. Never before had he felt time pass like that for the nation. He knew he would have to concentrate.

That day had been beautiful. The weather grew more beautiful as the day went on. When he finally left work the dusk around his house was cool and bright, with slender, temperate shadows. He had spent that day in a cycle. He'd spend an hour furiously searching the internet, typing in the acronyms of every news source he could think of—CNN, BBC, ABC, NBC, CBS, AP, NPR—and listening closely to the radio, where even the pop stations had given up their airwaves to the news. He craved information as a methodone for action. He called a friend who was a fireman to see if he knew more than the news did, if they had plans, if they needed help. They knew no more than he did, and told him they were set. He made his friend promise to call if they needed any help.

He'd spend the next hour trying ridiculously, bravely, to work. He read poems one by one, line by line, his blue pencil scratching out unclear words and too-clear motives or conclusions. He tried to do the job he was paid to do. He somehow felt, before he gave up and got on the Internet again, that this was the most patriotic thing he could do, the thing most in keeping with what his grandfathers would have done.

For days nothing was broadcast but news, moving pictures in which the all-encompassing cloud swelled and drifted over cities, above a roll of numbers, estimates, and possible facts. Even as the news departments ran out of things to say, and then gradually scaled back, and the programming readjusted, a tone remained for a while. The smug and the silly hid their faces and lowered their voices, but not for very long. Nothing had been asked of them, no sacrifice, no struggle. Now the nation was back to a bloated, prancing, half-assed normal. Now the urgent swagger was gone. Now Will went about his days with the news of armies vaguely known and mythologized, of small war after small duplicitous war, of a caste to do our fighting for us. Now much would be sacrificed, none of it nobly.

Sean had called on September 14, to let Will know he and Claire were safe. Claire had been uptown, near the park. She had stayed with friends in the Bronx, until they could drive her to her apartment in Jersey. Sean had been in Atlanta on business. He had spent anxious hours clutching his cell phone, but was ferociously grateful.

By the fence and the barricades most of the spectators spoke, discussed the last eight months. They debated the response. The cop leaned against the sawhorse, looking bored, staring at the sky, no longer listening. Will walked toward him, stepped around the barricades. The cop raised his hand, still looked bored. "Buddy ..."

Will looked the cop in the eye and held up the rose in his hand. He nodded slightly at the chain-link fence. The cop turned his palm away from Will and waved him on, and looked away. Holding the rose at the base of the bulb Will threaded the stem through the links.

Will stepped back, stood beside Sean and Claire. "You lucky son-of-a-bitch."

"Never thought I'd be glad to be in Atlanta," Sean said.

"Mary was here," Will said, "about a month before it happened. Visiting friends. She called me from here, from right here, a little after nine in the morning, to let me know she was all right."

"You lucky son-of-a-bitch."

"You think I don't think about that all the time?" Will glanced around the site. He remembered telling someone, before he left work that day, that these attacks were not acts of terrorism as much as acts of war. For all that their forebears had done to avoid it, war had come for them, too. He expected more attacks the next day. Those did not come, but others did, enough. The body politic could react as citizens or as customers. We could remain alert and intent, or we could be comfortable, lulled and distracted by luxuries, fairs, and the lives of our entertainers. We will be needed, Will said then. Those with access to the means of mass communication will have a duty, Will said, maybe not in those words. Maybe he hadn't said that at all; maybe he had just thought something along those lines. By the end of that day, though, he was jealous of those whose duty was to search, to save, to hunt down. He could smell smoke, could feel it scalding his nostrils, could feel the heat and adrenaline, could feel the weight of heavy tools in his hands. He almost quit his job and joined the Marines. He almost quit his job and drove up to New York with his well-worn work gloves. As the days went on, though, a purpose and a goal began to take shape in his mind. As the weeks went on Will wrote down every story that came to mind. He wrote down anecdotes he'd heard, family lore, urban legends, recollections. He translated them into travelling verses, fit for memorization, fit for a journey. As the months went on a work began to take shape. Someone would need to pay attention, to discern, describe and identify. Someone would need to stand unmoved in the marketplace until the best words came clear. Someone would need to tell the right stories well, the stories of survival and the monsters that had to be fought. He looked around the site, at the signs of work and removal, at the massive drop cloths draped over the adjacent buildings, at the square black tower across from him and the monstrous American flag it flew. He could have stayed there for hours, until after night had fallen, but he could see Sean and Claire backing away a step at a time. He stared out into the pit. He prepared himself to go.

Ed Southern was born in Winston-Salem, North Carolina, and began making up characters and stories shortly after. Before he was 10 years old, his mother had decided that "either this child is going to be a writer, or we're going to have to spend a fortune on therapy for him." (Whether that was a valid either/or proposition is still to be determined.)

Southern's previous work, all nonfiction, includes *The Jamestown Adventure*, *Voices of the American Revolution in the Carolinas*, and *Sports in the Carolinas*. He lives in Winston-Salem, and is executive director of the North Carolina Writers' Network.

Breinigsville, PA USA
01 September 2009
223392BV00001B/5/P